Look Under the Hawthorn

Look Under the Hawthorn

by

Ellen Frye

New Victoria Publishers, Inc.

Laser typeset in Palatino by the author.
Printed in the United States of America by Capital City Press.

Library of Congress Cataloging-in-Publication Data
Frye, Ellen, 1940–
   Look under the hawthorn

   I. Title
PS355.R9L6   1987   813'.54   87-60530
ISBN 0934678-12-X (pbk)

To the memory of Flossie Wright
1905—1987

Author's note

This first novel came out of a challenge from New Victoria Publishers to write a good lesbian novel. I am indebted to Claudia McKay of New Vic for that challenge and for subsequent challenges at every draft to make it better.

I am also indebted to Norma Kwestel, Louise Brill and Elaine Smith for careful editing and strong feedback; to Joan Larkin for her inspirational writers' workshop; to Terra Carta for permission to retell her ladder story; and to Marcie Pleasants for sharing with me her own adoption search experience.

1. Leaving the mud season behind

The distilled water of the Flowers of Hawthorne is not onely cooling, but drawing also, for it is afound by good experience that if Cloathes and Spunges be wet in sayd Water and applyed to any place whereinto Thornes, or Splinters, have entered and be there abiding, it will notably draw them forth; so that the Thorne giveth a Medicine for its owne pricking.

—Coles, 1657

The village square of Owensville, Vermont wasn't a square at all—it was a small triangle created by the fork of Clayborne Road dead-ending into the curve of Route 363. Clyde's General Store stood on one side of the triangle, the second side bordered a small pasture with three Dorset sheep badly in need of shearing. The Hockworth Inn, set back from the highway on a hill sloping up from the third side, reigned over the village like a Victorian duchess. Its three stories included a turret, a second story balcony and a dozen bay windows reflecting the sun. Iron mastiffs guarded worn stone steps that led to a great wooden door painted red. Inside, the hall opened onto a gracious parlour with Queen Anne chairs and a massive stone fireplace. Beyond double French doors, you could see a dining room with white table cloths and cut-glass chandeliers. The slender young desk clerk directed elegantly dressed couples on toward his maitre d' partner who showed them to their tables and took their wine orders with a flourish.

This was Sunday night, however, and through a small door to the right of the registration desk a different clientele entered. Women trouped in—alone, in couples or in groups—and nodded to the desk clerk, then made their way toward a door at the rear. Underneath the 'Employees Only' sign, a small business card read 'Rosamond LaRoque' in Garamond italic. Up a narrow set of stairs, down a hallway, through another door, and there it was: a wooden bar, a pool table, a juke box and a small dance floor. Behind the bar, a heavy-set woman with a prominent nose and grey hair polished shot glasses and set up drinks. Saturday and Sunday nights, the upstairs room at the Hockworth Inn was Rosie's bar. Not just a meeting place for all the dykes of central Vermont, the bar drew women from as far away as New York and Montreal. Dungarees and sweatshirts mingled with designer jeans and Italian import jackets, women's studies professors drank beer with backyard auto repair mechanics. On any given weekend there were no more than the usual number of 'shove it up your ass' comments. Only once had Rosie had to place her imposing frame between two pairs of fists.

Right now Rosie and several other women were listening intently to a small wiry carpenter with blazing eyes and gesticulating hands.

"So I'm balancing one gallon of paint, like this, and I go to take one step, and I say, mmm, no, I don't like that. So I take the gallon of paint, and I put my hand underneath it— I'm holding it like a waitress, right? And I got my paint brush in the other hand. And I go up, one, two, three, four.... And from around the house I hear Donna yelling to me, 'Korba, what are you doing anyway?' 'Don't talk to me, I have to concentrate.' Four, five.... And suddenly the ladder goes...whmp. It drops an inch, right? And it's not wiggily at all, it's really jammed in there between the house and the car, how did it go down an inch? So I'm ready to make the sixth step. Should I go forward or backward? I think I'm gonna go backwards. And the ladder goes...whmp! Down again, right? Oh, shit! So I said, what if I...uh...sprung off it. Cause I'm not really that high off the ground, and if I gave myself a little bend and then went boing, I could jump right off the ladder and land on the ground."

"With a full gallon of paint?" someone asked.

"With a full gallon of paint. So now I've got both feet on a rung. Okay, now, how do you do it on a diving board? You bring your weight up and then down and then bounce off. Okay, that's what I'm gonna do.

"Now the ladder had really jammed itself the second time down, I didn't realize that. And it's an aluminum ladder. So I go up and I go down and—*boing!* I'm flying through the air—straight up! I've already thrown my paint brush, I see the gallon of paint going down, I grab it by the handle—in air—I fall on the car, put the gallon of paint down, roll off the car and underneath another car."

"Painted the car instead of the house, huh?" said Rosie.

"Hey, I spilled some paint but not much. Ruined my brush though—it went right into a bucket of tar."

Out of the general laughter and applause, a voice boomed, "Well told, Korba. That calls for a round. Set 'em up, Rosie."

Edie Cafferty was speaking. Short, squarish and rugged, her reddish brown hair flecked with gray, she had ice blue eyes that could bore a hole right through you, then shift away as if they never saw you. She wore a faded blue denim work shirt, khakis and a worn brown leather jacket; steel-tipped shitkickers enclosed her feet. Anyone meeting her for the first time would lay odds that she was a mechanic or millhand or some other heavy dyke profession. In fact, she was a bookkeeper and had been so for the past twenty-five years of her life. Not that she couldn't use her hands for heavy labor. She was an ace with a welding gun and could put together two pieces of metal any way you wanted them—the seam would be invisible. But she did that for play—you couldn't make a living at it, welders were always getting laid off, you couldn't count on a steady paycheck. Bookkeeping was mostly boring, the pay was shit, but the job was secure. She'd been at this last one for twelve years. Anyway, she enjoyed the look on people's faces when she told them what she did for a living; they never knew what to say.

Rosie poured drinks all around. The attention of the barstoolers shifted to the pool table where a couple of known shots were chalking their cues. Edie turned her barstool with the rest of them and settled back, resting her elbows on the bar behind her. A babydyke beside her smiled sweetly at her and thanked her for the drink.

"She's a terrific storyteller, isn't she?" the young woman commented. "I mean, she makes it so real, it's almost like you were there. Is she a local dyke?"

"Korba?" replied Edie, turning to appraise the woman. "Yeah, if you get her going, she can go on for hours. This your first time here?"

Edie looked closely at the babydyke. Short-cropped blond hair, flat on top with a wispy pigtail behind. The usual babydyke uniform: patched jeans, a lavender teeshirt that read 'I can bleed forever' and four earrings in each ear, including three different double-women symbols. But the body was small, the face was cute with dimpled cheeks and a little bow mouth. Not exactly my type, thought Edie, but if you could imagine the hair long and the clothes a little femmier.... The babydyke was answering her question.

"Yeah, like I'm just passing through. I'm on the road these days, seeing the countryside. I was in Seattle and San Francisco last year, this year I'm doing the east coast. It's the first time I've gotten out into the country, though. It's really neat to see all these dykes in the woods. And your own lesbian bar, too."

The babydyke yawned. Edie's hand reached over to toy with the wispy pigtail.

"Traveling, huh? I thought I saw you with a backpack. If you're looking for a place to stay, I've got an extra bed. My place is just down the road, there's plenty of room."

The babydyke turned a sweet smile to her.

"Yeah? That'd be great. I was supposed to meet this friend from New York here, but it looks like she didn't make it. I'll get my stuff."

Rosie, wiping the bar behind Edie, overheard the exchange and raised an eyebrow. She hissed over Edie's shoulder,

"You keep picking 'em younger and younger, Edie, and they keep staying shorter and shorter. How long do you think this one will last?"

"Hey, some years the pickings are slim," Edie shot back. "Anyhow, under that babydyke swagger, she's real cute. Who knows, maybe she's looking to settle down."

As the two left the bar together, Edie felt her heart start its anticipatory dance. She'd been without a lover for almost six months now. Celibacy was advocated by Rosie, but it wasn't her idea of living. It was true, her lovers of the past few years hadn't seemed to stay very long. But then, women had changed a lot in the last thirty years. When she was in her young Boston bar scene days, roles were clear. There were pants and there were dresses, there were muscles and there were dainty lips. The women she liked identified themselves by the way they dressed and the way they talked. Edie, for her part, liked being the strong one, the one who paid for the drinks, who drove the car and ordered the dinner.

As for sex, Edie was a stonedyke and proud of it. Her fingers and tongue were skillful, she loved the feeling of sending another woman flying. Her own clit untouched, she took her pleasure in the pleasure of another. What was wrong with that?

Then the women's movement had come along and everything had changed. First, there were these stringy-haired young women who were always talking about the oppressor class of men. Yeah, well, men ran things, what else was new? The few men that Edie had known personally hadn't seemed so powerful. Her own dad had gotten up at four A.M every morning to go to work in a bakery and breathe flour twelve hours a day. He hadn't seemed very powerful to her, coughing and spitting in front of the television set every night.

Then the feminists had a harangue about how lesbians like her were aping men. Well, hell, maybe she enjoyed treating her friends to a drink now and then. And what if she did like women who made themselves up a bit? That didn't make her a man. What man ever gave pleasure the way she did? She'd fucked just once in her life, it was wham, bam, thank you ma'am. Men take pleasure, they don't give it. If you get some, too, okay, if you don't, tough. She, on the other hand, knew every erotic zone of a woman's body and knew how to stretch out the delight until finally, when the waves broke, the other woman's orgasm flowed in through her own fingertips and into her solid rock core. Nothing male about that.

Anyway, these days her type of woman was pretty hard to find. They all wore their hair cropped short and clumped and swaggered and swore. But Edie could usually still spot a femme-type, especially in younger women new to lesbianism.

Edie turned the truck onto a dirt road and bumped along for a quarter of a mile. She geared down to make the angle into the driveway, crossed the creek on the two-track wooden bridge and then bounced to a stop. It was pitch black as she helped the babydyke carry in her pack.

The babydyke, whose name turned out to be Dawn, seemed a little more eager than Edie'd expected. These young women didn't seem to understand that the chase is half the fun. Still, it was good to be in bed with a woman again, finding the familiar, yet unfamiliar places again, taking charge and giving, giving endless pleasure. As the babydyke's moans subsided, Edie lay back, feeling like a whole woman again. She drifted off to sleep.

Edie dreams. I'm driving a 1958 Fairlane Ford, a two-tone salmon pink hardtop convertible with big red nipple taillights. A little grey kitten beside me in the front seat is purring and chewing its tail. I know these back country roads like the back of my hand, and I take the curves fast with a flick of the squeal knob. At a left fork, the road climbs steeply, and the car almost stalls. Then we're over the top and flying down the other side, down into a lake, the car floating like an old Beetle, the kitten on my shoulder. The car disappears, and I feel the undertow sucking me down, down into the water. I see things I've never seen before—sea urchins and anemones that open and close. The little kitten swims next to me, chewing and biting my neck....

Edie, still half asleep, realized that something, someone was biting her neck—it was the babydyke nuzzling and kissing her while her fingers slipped down toward places untouched and untouchable.

"Hey! What the hell you think you're doing?"

The woman stopped and stared at her.

"Making love. Isn't that what we're here for?"

"Yeah, but I'm the one who makes the love, you're the one who flies."

The young woman cocked her head, thought for a moment and then rolled over.

"Jeez," she said, "Some of the women at Rosie's said you

9

were a stonedyke. I heard the term before, but I didn't know what it meant, and those women were so heavy-duty, I didn't want them to know how dumb I was. Now I guess I'm finding out."

"You got any problems with it?"

"I guess not. I like flying, if you want to do all the work."

Once, twice, three more times Edie piloted the young woman's flight. Then they fell back exhausted and slept.

The next morning, Edie rolled out of bed feeling like a million dollars. She grinned at the sight of the sleeping child-woman. Rosie was right, she was pretty young, looked barely out of her teens. Ah, but there was so much to teach her. Edie tried to remember where she'd stowed her box of erotica—the special oils, the vibrator with the rotating dildo attachment. Plans bounced around her head as a fluffy cheese omelet took shape under her deft hands. She became aware of two dark eyes watching her from the bed.

"Hey, you're awake just in time. Breakfast will be served in the main dining room just as soon as I can get rid of the kitchen and the bedroom. Move over here," she commanded.

Edie rolled down a slatted wooden blind to hide the stovetop-sink-refrigerator combination. Then, as Dawn hopped on one foot with the bedquilt wrapped around her, she grasped a handle at the foot of the bed and hoisted it up until a strong spring took it the rest of the way into the wall.

"A Murphy bed!" cried Dawn, delighted. "My grandmother told me about them. I never really believed they existed. Now, where's the john?"

"You see that old blue Beetle?" Edie pointed out the window. "If you open the right door, you'll find a two-seater. You have a choice of a mountain view or one facing the cows in the pasture. Take your pick depending on what you'd like to look at while you shit. If you're a reader, there's a little library under the dash where the steering wheel used to be. The tape deck works, too—I juiced up the battery yesterday."

"Awesome," said Dawn as she came back in. "This place is awesome. How'd you do it?"

"Oh, I know a little welding," Edie responded casually. "I started out with a railroad flatcar that had derailed itself into a gully. It sat there for years until the farmer who owned the gully decided he wanted to dam it up to make a lake. He said I could have the flatcar for the hauling. I got him to sell me an acre to put it on and put out the word that anybody who wanted to junk a wreck could. Before the week was out, I had two Fords, a Chevy, a Pontiac and a Hudson. I started welding them together just for fun, and little by little it grew into a house, so I moved in. Now I just add a little here or there whenever I get the materials. I call her my Tin Lizzie. I'll give you the tour after breakfast."

The contours of the multicolored structure were determined by the fenders, roofs and hoods of a dozen cars welded together. The kitchen window was made of two Buick doors that could be rolled down easily whenever you wanted to dump seed into the muffler bird feeder just outside. In the living room, two windshields and frames welded bottom to bottom with back windows on either side looked south over the pasture and the creek. The structure was winter-tight, too. Walls and floors were insulated and panelled with old barn siding. The ceiling was covered with Victorian molded tin squares rescued from a remodeling job undertaken by a New York couple who thought tin was junk. Everything was neat and orderly. With the Murphy bed up and the kitchen stashed behind its blind, the house was divided neatly into two large rooms separated by a brick hearth and a wood stove. A sofa and two chairs, handmade from hickory saplings, filled one room. The other room held a spool table lit by a hanging lamp made of the bottoms of coke bottles. A rough-cut pine bookcase full of records and a large stereo cabinet completed the decor.

"Jeez," said Dawn, fingering the bookcase as she drank her coffee, "you made all of this yourself? The house, the furniture, everything?"

"Yeah, well, you gotta have something to keep yourself busy in the wintertime, or else you'll go crazy. Bring your coffee cup, I'll show you around outside."

The house was set at an angle at the foot of a hill facing south. To the east, a small garden plot had been neatly put to bed last fall under a blanket of leaves. Beyond that, Jersey cows grazed in the neighboring pasture. Behind the house, tucked under the hill, the blue Beetle outhouse was flanked by two large maples. To the west was the graveyard. Engines, carburetors, mufflers and radiators grew out of the weeds along with half a dozen frames stripped of doors, windows, fenders and hoods.

The hillside behind the house was still brown with spring growth just beginning to poke through the rocky soil. At the top of the hill, Edie named the different mountains you could see beyond the valley, while Dawn picked early spring flowers. She started to break off the budding leaf of the lone tree on the hill when she jumped back suddenly.

"Ouch! It bit me. What is it?"

"That's a hawthorn," laughed Edie. "Look, the thorns are only at the ends of the branches. It'll flower pink in a few weeks, and later there'll be red berries with a hard nut inside. Ma used to call me her little hawthorn whenever I got too prickly."

The spring sun was melting the last of the snow on the surrounding mountains. Edie felt that this spring was her spring, her time for renewal. Time to get back into loving and living. This young woman was a real beauty, especially

12

if she could get her to grow her hair out a bit. She looked like she'd been traveling awhile, she needed a little taking care of. TLC was an Edie specialty, and she was more than ready for the giving. It was going to be a great mud season.

The week following, Edie sailed through her work, humming and chuckling to herself. She wore a fresh shirt to work every day and made sure the crease in her chinos was razor sharp. Instead of her usual mutter directed toward her computer, she set up a rhythm punching the terminal keys. She didn't even say 'shit' when she hit the wrong key and sent an hour's worth of figures into oblivion.

Her office was a cubicle in a corner with a single window that looked over the company parking lot. Last year she'd had a whole room with a mountain view on the other side of the building, but that was when she'd been responsible for the whole accounting operation. The company was having a growth spurt now, and they'd brought in a comptroller, a young pup just out of college with rosy cheeks that looked like maybe they sprouted enough for him to shave once a week. He was the one responsible for bringing in the PCs and the automated spreadsheets. He'd told her she could throw away her pencil and pink pearl eraser, that everything could be done by computer. But it took twice as long now to enter the figures for the disbursement journal and run the calculation formulas than it had to just tick them off with a pencil and total the balance with her old adding machine. Especially when the printer standing right outside her door jarred her every time it starting grinding out its unending roll of perforated paper.

The young pup Chad noticed Edie's merry mood and tried to joke about how there must be a new man in her life. Edie could imagine his management textbook instructing him on the benefits of joking with his employees to set them at ease. No doubt there was an index of jokes he could consult every morning. Usually his cracks—which ran in the vein of teaching old dogs new tricks, chuckle, chuckle—brought a suppressed snarl from Edie which would send him scurrying to the receptionist who could giggle and toss her dark pony tail. These days, Edie simply raised an eyebrow and continued punching the terminal keys. Chad seemed relieved and grateful.

Every day at five o'clock, she shut down the machines, smoothed the crease in her chinos, threw on her old tweed jacket, and bolted for the door. By 5:25 she was flinging open the door and falling into the arms of Dawn.

Dawn Bettychild was the whole name.

"What kinda name is that?" she had asked the second night. Dawn had given her a long ramble about the patriarchy, and how we have to give ourselves names that belong to us, that tell us who we are. And she'd chosen Dawn because she felt a new day for women was dawning and Bettychild to honor her mother who'd given up her name and her self when she married her father who was an operations manager for a high tech company in Chicago. He beat her mother whenever he drank, which was whenever the company was in trouble, which was a lot. But her mother stuck by him, said he was basically a good man, and where would she go if she left him? She, Dawn, had left when she was sixteen and had been on the

15

road ever since.

"And how long is that?" asked Edie.

"Five years next month. I'm never going back. I miss my baby sister sometimes. Wish I could bring her with me, but she's only eleven, so my father'd probably have me arrested for kidnapping or something. I call Mom sometimes—collect, that bastard can afford it—and she keeps telling me how things are better now, the company's doing well, and he doesn't drink as much as he used to and doesn't hit her hardly at all. She says Josie's doing okay although she won't eat and is skinny as a rail. It doesn't sound to me like things are going that great."

Dawn rolled over on her side and twirled her pigtail.

"What have you been doing all this time on the road?" asked Edie. She couldn't imagine leaving her home and just traveling from one place to another.

"After I left home," Dawn answered, "I spent a coupla years with this woman who trained horses for the Olympic teams."

She giggled and blushed.

"I guess you could say I like older women, huh? But I do, you've got so much for me to learn from. Anyway, I went around the country with her on her training trips. But then she kinda got to be a drag, she got so jealous whenever I so much as talked to another woman, so I split. I like traveling alone now. I get to meet all these great women and see how women are making it happen all over the country. I love just dropping into a bar where I don't know anybody and finding new friends. Sisterhood is really neat."

Edie liked to listen to the patter. She'd never spent much time with the babydykes, much as she liked to watch them dance at Rosie's. Most of them seemed like they came from another planet. All that toughness—

cigarettes hanging from their lower lips, calling each other 'cunts'—it didn't quite fit their smooth baby faces. Besides, they usually ignored her. Looked at her blankly if she tried to start a conversation.

"Sometimes I think they don't even see us," she joked to Rosie. But she knew it wasn't a joke. It really pissed her that these same young women who driveled on about reclaiming women's history were incapable of recognizing any woman who'd actually lived through some of it.

She forgot her gripes in the arms of Dawn. A silly name, maybe, but Lord how the child could fly. Edie hadn't had so much sex in years. Dawn never seemed to get enough, she kept going and going, one orgasm after another. Edie was proud that she never tired herself.

This Friday afternoon she started clockwatching right after lunch. Kept her nose glued to the terminal screen for as long as she could stand, then couldn't believe only ten minutes had passed since she'd last looked. Her head was full of anticipation for the weekend. Two full days of lovemaking, maybe dinner at the new SurfnTurf, a drive up Alben's Gore, and evenings at Rosie's. Who knows, she might even dance herself. She didn't usually feel that comfortable dancing, but right now she felt she could do anything.

The moment Edie stepped inside the trailer, she knew it was over. The bulging knapsack was propped by the door, Dawn was hacking away at her hair with a pair of scissors. Edie closed the door and dropped into the rocker. Dawn looked at her with a nervous defiance. Neither of them spoke.

Edie got up and poured herself a tumbler of Jack Daniels.

"There's a steak house down the road," she said finally. "The salad bar's pretty good for you. Myself, I think I

17

need to sink my teeth into something medium rare."

Dawn's body relaxed. She moved to where Edie was standing and put her arms around her.

"You know that's who I am, I gotta keep moving. I got a friend in Portland, I'll stay there tomorrow night, then move on up the coast and see if I can land a waitress job in one of the tourist joints. It's good money for the summer, and I've never seen the Maine coast...."

Edie tossed off her drink and took Dawn by the arm.

"Come on, lassie, my stomach's growling. Let's go eat."

The early morning fog still hung over the valley when Edie set Dawn down at the entrance to the interstate. Back home, she puttered in the garden. There wasn't much to do. The plot was small, and it was too early to plant. Mostly she spudded dandelions and cut out some of the dead branches on the old lilac.

She'd hardly known Dawn, spent less than a week with her, but she felt as empty as when Frances had left. Or Dorothy. Or June. Yegods, she thought, let's not start a litany of lost lovers.

By nightfall she was completely out of sorts. She poured herself a double shot of bourbon and put on a Betty Carter tape. But both the music and the whiskey seemed sour. She pulled records out at random—Carmen MacRae, Marian McPartland, Anita O'Day, all good women who'd hacked it in the male world of jazz. It was flat, she'd heard every record a hundred times. Her ears stubbornly refused to listen.

She took a book off her bookshelf, but she didn't want to read another Jane Rule. She didn't want to read about somebody else's life. She'd been doing that all her life. Always somebody else out there doing the interesting things, going the interesting places. Ten years she'd spent in this damn tin box. Twelve years driveling figures into Industrial Tools, Inc. Twenty years in this suffocating little community. She flung the book at the wall. Hannah jumped onto the windowsill, switching her long black tail and stared disdainfully. Edie glowered back.

"Goddammit, Edie," she muttered to herself, "your butt's got green mold. No wonder Dawn hot-footed it out of here."

She threw on her jacket and left.

Sitting on her regular barstool at Rosie's, she swirled her ice cubes and watched the young crowd party.

"Where's the little cutie you left here with last weekend?" Rosie teased. "She looked young enough to be your daughter."

"Younger," growled Edie. "My daughter would've been thirty-two this month." Edie startled herself. Where the hell had that come from?

"You got a kid, Edie? I never knew that."

"Well, I did. Or still do, I suppose. Had her when I was sixteen. Ma liked to kill me when she found out. Beat me up one side and down the other, called me seventeen different kinds of slut. Packed me off to a home for unwed mothers. The sisters there prayed for my soul 'til I didn't know if I was vomiting from morning sickness or moral nausea. When I told them I wanted to keep the kid, they about died of shock and prayed even harder. I managed to get out one night, stole some money from the chapel poor box—figured I was the poor one. Then I walked the five miles into town and shipped out on the next Greyhound to Boston."

Edie stopped and drained her glass. Rosie poured her another, then leaned her elbows on the bar and cocked her head.

"So what happened then?" she asked.

"I had this aunt in Charlestown," Edie continued. "You shoulda seen the look on her face when I rang the bell, belly big as a basketball. She was pretty game, though. She didn't send me back to the nuns anyway. But she did talk me into giving the kid up—it would grow up with the bastard stigma, how was I gonna support it, et cetera, et cetera."

Edie drank again and rattled her ice cubes. Rosie obliged with another shot.

"So you gave her up, huh? Must of been tough."

"Well, yes and no. I signed all the papers this lawyer and social worker shoved at me. But when my time came closer, something in me started balking. I sniveled and I sighed. Aunt Flo got snappy. Then one night I took twenty bucks from her wallet, got up at daybreak the next morning, and took off again. There weren't any buses at that hour, so I hoofed it across the bridge. Hopped the first bus that came along and took it to the end of the line. Then walked some more. I ended up somewhere in Watertown in a rooming house run by a Lithuanian woman and her two daughters."

"Sounds like you were pretty tough for a sixteen-year-old."

"Well, tough I don't know. But stubborn, yes. I never had a damn thing of my own as a kid except a kitten that got run over by a truck. Mostly all we got was a licking whenever we stepped out of line. Which we all did regularly. My sister and I'd get grounded for back-talking, and we'd lie in bed and wait for them to go to sleep. Then I'd climb out the window onto the porch roof—it was over about four feet, but if I swung my legs right I could hit it easy. One time I missed it and put a foot through my folks' bedroom window. There was real hell to pay that time."

Edie chuckled as she remembered the licking she got. Her mother made her father administer it, but he kept coughing every couple of licks and had to stop and catch his breath. A licking from her mother was no laughing matter, but her father couldn't carry it off and didn't seem to care. Edie went on.

"Mostly we got out without too much trouble and scooted off down to the corner of South Main and Gates. My sister'd go screw her boyfriend, but I hung out around the Coolidge Hotel and listened to the jazz coming out the side door. White River Junction was a real railroad town in those days—smoky, sooty and grimy. But a lot of name bands stopped off to do a one-night stand on their way from New York to Montreal.

"Anyway, one night my sister's boyfriend had a cousin with him, and they talked me into going inside with them. The boys were old enough, but I don't know how they got us inside—the hotel was usually pretty strict about letting minors in. Anyway, I was all bug-eyed looking at the musicians up close, and I drank whatever they put in front of me. The rest is the usual crap—girl gets drunk, boy knocks her up and disappears. Well, that was fine and dandy with me, he was a jerk. But that thing in my belly—that was mine, all mine. And the bigger I got, the surer I was that nobody else was gonna have it."

Edie polished off her glass again and shoved it across the bar. She was surprised at herself. She hadn't told this story to anyone ever, had mostly forgotten it herself. She'd come in feeling sorry for herself about Dawn, and suddenly this old stuff had popped out. What the hell, it was a good story, and Rosie was a good ear. It didn't mean anything to her anyway after all these years.

She went on. A couple of other semi-familiar faces had moved closer to hear. Edie swilled her drink and settled into the story. She told how the Lithuanian landlady had helped her deliver, and how she had left the kid with her during the day while she trekked halfway across town to the girl friday job that paid forty dollars a week. She'd named the kid Sarah, but she hardly ever saw her awake. Except in the middle of the night when she screamed for her bottle. And then wouldn't go back to sleep for hours.

Brought up poor and proud, Edie'd been determined to pay her aunt back. So when she'd sent the postal order, she had dutifully filled in her name and address. Aunt Flo had been on the doorstep in a fury by return mail. It was January. Aunt Flo had ranted about how the baby was sick because the room was damp and unheated. What's more, Edie had signed the papers, it was illegal for her to keep the child.

"I was exhausted from being sick myself and sitting up nights with Sarah and working a six-day week. But I dug in and told her they couldn't have her, I didn't care what I'd signed. Sarah was screaming and coughing, the landlady and her two daughters were jabbering away in Lithuanian, Aunt Flo was yelling that the law was the law.

"Then this couple appeared in the doorway. Brown suits and hatchet faces. The kind that wouldn't say 'shit' if their mouths were full of it. The man waved his arm and silenced us all. Well, Sarah didn't stop crying, but the rest of us turned into little stone statues. He announced that he was the lawyer for the agency and some crap about the best interests of the child and the court order, and before I knew it, the woman had pried Sarah out of my arms, and they were all gone."

Edie drank up and wiped her mouth with the back of her hand. She was suddenly exhausted.

"Those sons of bitches. How could they pull a stunt like

that? It couldn't've been legal."

"For all I know it wasn't. I didn't see my Aunt Flo for two years. When I did, neither of us mentioned it. Hell, I suppose they were right, I couldn't have taken care of the kid. Not on forty bucks a week and no likelihood of making any more."

"Did you ever try to find her?" This came from one of the other listeners, a younger woman, short and round with frizzy hair.

"Find her? Jesus Christ, why would I want to find her? She has her own life, a helluva lot better than anything I could've given her. I had my chance and I blew it." Edie, surprised at her own vehemence, took another drink.

"Well," the woman persisted, "it sounds like you still have some anger about it. For all you know, she may, too. If you two could get together, you might be able to help each other work through it."

Edie just wanted to sleep, but something inside her broke.

"Oh kee-rist, spare me the psychobabble. What the sweet fuck do you know about how I feel? Or how she feels? Who the hell do you think you are? Who asked you to listen? Who asked you to analyze my life? You god-damn little twerp, you think you know so much, you don't know shit. Go take a flying fuck at the moon, why don't you...."

Edie felt Rosie's firm grip on her elbow.

"Come on, Edie, I've got a spare bed. You'll have a little nap, and then I'll drive you home."

Edie dreams. I'm standing in a hillside pasture, looking at a stone wall broken by frost heaves. I try to push one of the boulders back into place, but it rolls down the hill and into the creek. The creek is full from springtime flooding, the water is moving fast. A little girl on the other side is waving at me, saying something, but I can't hear it. I start over the bridge, but halfway across I see it's collapsed into the water. A bunch of women are swimming in the creek, and one of them calls to me to join them, but I'm not wearing the right clothes. She reaches up and pulls me in. We splash around, then we're making love. She's biting my ear just like Dawn and....

"Jesus wept!" Edie grunted as she came out of it. "It's that goddamn frizzy-headed psychologizing twerp again!"

"Well, whoever it was, it must've felt good." Rosie grinned as she pushed a cup of black coffee at her. "Here, this should take the hair off your teeth."

Edie sat up and groaned. "I musta put on a real load last night. Looks like I didn't even make it home."

"You don't look so great this morning either. You want to call in sick from here?"

Edie closed her eyes while she drank the coffee. Her brows kept furling and unfurling. Sometimes she'd snort and then wince and take another deep draft. When the cup was empty, she set it down deliberately and walked across the room to the phone.

"Chad Burdock, please. ... Hello, Chad? Edie Cafferty. I thought I'd let you know that I'm going to start my two-week vacation today. ... Well, yes, as a matter of fact, I can. Because that same two weeks is my notice. ... That's right, Chad, dear. You can take that One-Two-Three program and shove it up your dainty rosebud ass, you can rev up that rackety-jack printer machine and let it roll forever, you can blow your jokes out your ass all day long, I won't say a word, I won't even be there. Just put my paycheck into the mail and go ahead and hire somebody with pointy tits and fuck-me heels."

Edie held the sputtering receiver away from her for a moment and then placed it gently on the hook.

"Well, I'll be goddamned!" breathed Rosie.

"You and me both," countered Edie and poured herself another cup of coffee.

"Moving Sale. Hand-made furniture, kitchen ware, clothes, books, welding tools, garden tools. Everything priced to go." Rosie read the sign aloud as she took it down. "And I guess it was, it sure looks like everything went. I take it these boxes of records you set aside you want to store with me."

"Yeah, I'd appreciate it if you'd keep 'em dry. That jazz collection is the one thing I don't want to give up. I've got stuff in there from way back, old seventy-eights a friend of mine gave me when I was a kid. Don't know when I'll ever listen to them again, but I sure as hell don't want to let them go." Edie frowned as she punched her calculator and jotted down some figures. "Well, that's it, then. That's everything. At age forty-eight, I'm worth exactly five thousand, five hundred dollars and some change."

"That's it for everything?"

"Yeah. I sold the acre back to Farmer Eddie for the same fifteen hundred I paid for it. I spent two-fifty on that truck bed camper last night. I made eight hundred and fifty one dollars today, and my last paycheck will be four eighty-seven twenty-five. I got eleven hundred and forty-seven dollars in my savings account and six hundred ninety eighty-five in checking, and I'll be getting three thousand and something out of that silly pension plan they got at work. So that's it, a little over fifty-five hundred."

"God, Edie," said Rosie. "How long have I known you? Twenty, twenty-five years? And I've never known you to do a single impulsive thing. Ever. You're steady as a rock, drinking Jack Daniels in my bar every Saturday and Sunday night, spending your vacations working on your house, I'll bet you haven't taken a sick day in years. Now suddenly, you throw up your job, you sell this monument and everything in it, just like that, no warning at all. What's going on? Are you serious about this search for your daughter?"

"I guess I am, I seem to be going, don't I? I don't know why, I never thought about her before. But right now it just seems like that's what I got to do. And I can't do it in Owensville, Vermont. She's out there somewhere, Rosie, maybe in Boston, maybe in California, who knows? I don't know about impulsive, maybe that's what I'm gonna be in the second half of my life. Combine it with my stubborn, and maybe I'll never settle down again."

"Well, I wouldn't want to stop you, even if I could. I think it's great you're gonna get out of here and see the world. I mean, the French in me says you're crazy to sell the house you spent the last ten years of your life creating with your own two hands to somebody who'll probably bulldoze it into oblivion. Stay put, hang on to what you've got, it says. But the Indian in me says, You're right, possessions are nothing, connections are everything. Go on out there and make them if you possibly can. Where are you going first?"

"I'll start with Aunt Flo. After thirty-two years we ought to be able to talk about it. She's the only one that even knows the name of the agency. I suppose it's long gone, but I gotta start somewhere."

"And where's Aunt Flo now?"

"Same place she's been all along. Same two grubby rooms in grubby Charlestown, same grubby job at a grubby import/export firm, probably the same grubby salary. She should of retired years ago, but the company never bothered with a pension plan. She wouldn't know what to do with herself anyway. Her friends have either moved away or died, and she never was one for hobbies. I haven't seen her in ten years, but we've kept up with Christmas cards. It'll be real interesting to hear what she has to say about all this."

Edie looked around. The violets were beginning to color the hillside behind the house, the hawthorn tree at the top was in full bloom. The little plot wasn't all bad, it'd been real nice, in fact. She picked up Hannah.

"Take good care of her, Rosie. She's loud and funny looking, but she's got a good heart. If you don't feed her too much, she won't get much fatter. Anyway, she'll clean out the mice in your cellar. When they're all gone, she'll bring home dead leaves."

"She's gonna miss you, Edie." Rosie took the cat and the cat food. "Hell, I'm gonna miss you. Don't forget to come home sometime. There's always a bed."

Edie hugged her. "Don't worry. Fifty-five hundred dollars won't go that far. It's probably a wild goose chase anyway. But I'm long overdue for a change."

Each woman climbed into her own car. They sat there for several minutes, motors running. Then the pickup rolled down the driveway and turned right, while the little blue Maverick followed and turned left. Hannah put her paws up on the window and yowled.

"Yeah, little bit, we're gonna miss her. Go on and yowl for both of us."

2. One river flows into another

Halfway to Boston, it hit her. Here she was, steady-as-a-rock Edie Cafferty, having just thrown up her job and sold all her possessions to ramble God knows where in search of a thirty-two-year-old ghost whose features had long since faded into the atmosphere. It was contrary to her fundamental nature. Edie Cafferty was a homebody who didn't like traveling, everybody knew that. Rebellious maybe as a kid, but you had to be in White River where you could either go to church or hang out with the railroad crowd.

Her mind rolled back over the twenty-odd years she'd spent in Owensville. She'd come there with Frances after ten years on the Boston bar scene. In those days everyone had done the butch/femme number. She'd had a tuxedo to Frances' black net stockings. After they'd been together a few years, they'd found they preferred playing cards with Aunt Flo and Charlene. Eventually Frances had said, "Let's go live in Vermont." Edie had responded, "No, thanks, I've already been," but she knew she, too, wanted a home, a real house with maybe sixteen cats.

Well, Edie thought, it lasted ten years, more than most. They'd lived in somebody's barn for a couple of years, then they'd moved into an old farmhouse a few miles

31

outside of Owensville. She'd thought they were both happy, hadn't had a clue that Frances was leaving until she came home from work one day and found her packing her bags. She'd heard all Frances' talk about going to law school, but hell, neither one of them had ever finished high school, Edie couldn't see how her salary could cover tuition payments. Then Frances had met a woman with money and a college degree. Next thing Edie knew she was alone. Last time she'd heard, Frances was up in Montpelier working for a senator.

By the time Edie hit 93 South, she'd reviewed all the women of her life. It seemed that each relationship had been a little bit shorter than the last. They always started out with a lot of sex and passion, then settled down to meat loaf and mashed potatoes. There never seemed to be any problem with getting along, Edie had a steady job and paid the bills. Owensville didn't provide much in the way of excitement, but there was always a handful of dykes scattered among the hills you could get together to play poker with. Rosie had started her bar by renting the grange once a month and throwing a BYO dance. There were a couple of steak houses to choose from and in the summertime a drive-in movie. Edie would find herself a sweetie and start settling in, getting used to the rhythm of married life, things would be going along just fine and then suddenly, poof, the woman would be up and gone. If Dawn was any indication of the general trend, she'd soon be down to one-night stands. Oh, well, there's more to life than sex, Edie thought. Look at Rosie, she's been celibate for years, and she really enjoys life. Says she's outgrown all that heavy breathing shit. On the other hand, sex makes you really come alive, there's nothing else like it.

Edie's thoughts turned to the task at hand. A woman was out there, her own flesh and blood. She could almost still feel the soft reddish fuzz of Sarah's baby head, smell the baby powder she'd put on her bottom. Edie wasn't sure where the compulsion was coming from, but it was there, burning strong. She didn't suppose Sarah knew anything about her, maybe didn't know she even existed, maybe didn't care. It didn't matter. Edie was as determined as she'd been the day she took the twenty bucks from Aunt Flo and trudged off to Watertown. Only this time she'd be damn sure nobody would talk her out of it.

The last half-hour coming into Boston, Edie rehearsed what she was going to tell Aunt Flo. They'd never been real close—the Sarah incident had kept Edie wary for years. By the time she'd forgiven Aunt Flo for that, she'd been heavy into her bulldagger role—drinking and partying and biking. Her family had pretty much disowned her when she showed up at her father's wake shirtless, with a black leather vest and a tattoo on her bicep. Then her mother had died, the family had scattered, and she'd lost track of most of them, even her sister who'd moved out west. She'd kept in touch with Aunt Flo because, she wasn't sure why, maybe because Aunt Flo never asked questions. And she could always count on a meal and a good game of cards there.

For years, Edie had dropped in every two or three months. Aunt Flo would update her on what was happening with the various branches of the family. When Edie had met Frances, the first thing she'd done was take her to meet Aunt Flo. The two of them had gotten along great, and after that they'd spent a fair amount of time together. When Frances and Edie had moved to Owensville, Frances had kept up a correspondence with Aunt Flo, and they'd visited two or three times a year. But after Frances left, Edie almost never went to Boston. Aunt Flo eventually became a Christmas card in her life.

Aunt Flo's apartment was on the third floor of a yellow brick building next to a Shell station. Edie climbed the stairs, wondering if Aunt Flo had gotten the post card she'd mailed the day before yesterday. The paint was peeling on the stair railing, mild graffiti dotted the walls. The lathing over Aunt Flo's door showed through the broken plaster. Edie was about to knock when Aunt Flo opened the door. Aunt Flo hadn't changed a bit in the ten years since Edie last saw her. She'd lost a few pounds from her short square frame, but she still looked strong. She was wearing the same flowered apron over the same patterned house dress Edie'd last seen her in, and her bright blue eyes peered sharply through her rimless glasses. They embraced awkwardly. Then Aunt Flo stepped back and drew Edie inside.

"I heard you on the stairs," she said. "I'd recognize that footfall of yours anywhere, Edie. Here, let me look at you. You've hardly changed. You take after the Cafferty side for sure—red hair 'til fifty."

Aunt Flo bustled to the stove and lifted the lid on a large cast iron pot.

"I've got some good Irish stew here waiting for you. You didn't eat yet, did you? Sit down, I'll serve you."

Edie sat obediently at the kitchen table with its familiar blue checkered oilcloth. Nothing had changed here at all. The table was set with the same blue patterned china she'd eaten off of years ago, the Irish stew gave off the same thick smell. A single overhead light threw a yellowish hue over the wallpaper and cast shadows into the corners of the small room.

"I was so pleased to get your card, Edie," continued Aunt Flo. "I keep thinking I'll go visit you in Vermont, but I never do. I used to visit when you were a little girl, but it always seems like such a long journey."

"There're interstates now, Aunt Flo," said Edie, between bites. "It only takes a couple of hours."

"I know. Somehow I never get around to it."

"Well, I'm not one to talk, I haven't visited you either." Edie chewed on a gristly piece of meat.

"And what brings you here now, Edie?" asked Aunt

Flo. "Is it a short or long visit?"

Edie ducked her head. All her explanations in the truck had seemed solid. But now, sitting face to face with Aunt Flo, she couldn't bring herself to talk about how she was chasing a ghost. She cleared her throat a couple of times, coughed, and then sat staring into the stew.

"You always were a difficult child, Edie. No one ever knew what you were thinking or what you were likely to do. I never envied my sister-in-law. Your grandmother used to try to comfort me because all my sisters had husbands and families and I was left on the shelf. But every time I thought about your mother and your father and you six kids up there in White River, I knew I was the lucky one. You can say what you like about working for Allied Imports, but it's a damn better job than taking care of a sick man and six unruly kids in a god-forsaken railroad town."

Edie looked at Aunt Flo out of the corner of her eye. She'd lived on her own all her life. Her friends had always been women like her, self-supporting, none of them married, some of them even lived together. It suddenly hit Edie that Aunt Flo might have been—might be—a lesbian! Maybe Aunt Flo had disapproved of her early dyke days only because of the boozing and brawling. Edie realized that, like most younger relatives, she'd never asked Aunt Flo about her life. Well, that was partly the family style—don't ask personal questions, never show feelings. Now Edie was curious, really curious to know just how Aunt Flo had come to choose her life.

"Well," Aunt Flo began, "let's see. I was twenty-three when the war broke out. My closest sister—your Aunt Sally—was twenty-one. Your father—he was three years older than me—he married your mother in 'thirty-four. So when they bombed Pearl Harbor, you were three, I think, and your sister was six. Anyway, Sally and I both got jobs in the munitions factory. Between the two of us, we were

35

bringing home a pretty fair paycheck. Sally wasn't too happy about the war taking all the boys away—she'd been a real fine looking girl. You never saw that—she got worn down pretty quick when she started having babies. But then she was a fine looking girl. Anyway, we were bringing home all this money and putting food on the table and having left over to buy everybody new shoes, and, truth be known, I didn't mind the war one bit. I never had a beau and never wanted one. So if they all went off to war, it was fine with me. And I thought working in the factory was good fun. It was just about all women. We told jokes and smoked cigarettes on our breaks and went to the movies together on Saturday nights."

Aunt Flo got up and put the burner on under the coffeepot.

"Well, of course, now I know how badly we were exploited," she said as she waited for the pot to boil. "They got us for half the pay they'd of had to give men. But then…well, nobody amongst the Cafferties had worked in any regular fashion during the depression. If you got chicken and dumplings on a Sunday, you had to relish every bit, because you never knew when you'd see a drumstick again."

She poured two cups and brought them back to the table.

"So there we were for four years. A lot of food was rationed, but what was available you could afford. Then they dropped the bomb. The boys came home, and Sally got swept off her feet by a navy man. Along with just about everybody else. The factory went back to making ships' parts, the boys married the girls and took over their jobs. At twice the pay. Some of us didn't get swept off our feet and stayed on, but it wasn't the same. No more jokes and cigarette breaks. The men got real nasty sometimes. And one by one, we all got laid off. Our jobs got reclassified, they said women couldn't do the new jobs. When I was offered the position at Allied Imports, I was really grateful even though the pay was a lot less. Your grandmother could be a real nag when it came to why I didn't have a beau. Anyway, my girlfriend and I—you remember her, Charlene Gooding, we used to play bridge with you and Frances. Well, Charlene and I found an apartment here in Charlestown, just a few blocks from here. And we set up housekeeping together."

Edie remembered Charlene. She had been tall and elegant, and she had loved to shatter the elegance with the most raucous laugh you'd ever heard. Now Edie was really curious. She was halfway to asking straight out when she looked at Aunt Flo and stopped short. Wait a minute, Edie, she said to herself. This is Aunt Flo you're talking to, not some dyke at Rosie's. What difference does it make whether they slept together or not? Instead she said,

"I remember Charlene. But you haven't mentioned her in any of your Christmas cards recently. Where is she?"

Aunt Flo stared into her cup. "She got an inheritance, oh, it must be six or seven years ago. It wasn't much, but she said she'd always wanted to see the world. She asked me to go with her, but I just couldn't see it, two old ladies in Paris. So she went by herself. Quit her job, gave up her apartment, packed her bags and left. I went to the airport with her. She said she'd be back when the money ran out. Six months, a year at the most. But she's never come back, not even for a visit. She's living in Greece now, she's a governess for some rich Athenians. She writes faithfully and tells me I should come and visit. Sometimes I think I should, but...."

Aunt Flo stopped and looked at the wall clock. "Land, child, it's eleven o'clock. We've been talking all night. Here, we'll leave the dishes and wash up tomorrow. I'll leave you to make up the couch, you know where the sheets are."

Lying in the dark, Edie listened to the traffic outside

and thought about Aunt Flo. She wondered what was stopping her going to Greece to live with Charlene. Social security didn't cover shit here, but over there she could probably live on it okay. Of course, Edie knew what was stopping her, the same thing that had stopped Edie from leaving Owensville for twenty years, the moulty hen syndrome. Set on the nest long after the eggs have gone rotten just because nest-setting is the only thing you know how to do.

E die spent a good part of the first week just getting used to Boston again. Driving was the same old nightmare of dodging lunatics and having parking tickets slapped on your windshield the instant the meter popped. She mostly left the truck on the street outside Aunt Flo's and took the bus into the city. She spent a lot of time walking around Beacon Hill, avoiding the dog shit whenever possible. The little patisseries on Charles Street offered lots of take-out goodies, and she often lunched in the Public Garden where she watched the swanboats ferry tourists around the pond.

Edie found herself looking at women in a way she'd never done before. She'd always been a looker. But now, instead of typing what she saw and thinking about how she might put the make on her, she looked first to see whether a woman was in the early thirties age bracket. Then she looked for signs. Just what she was looking for she didn't know. The Cafferties didn't have any peculiarly identifying features except for the reddish-brown hair she shared with her dad and two of her brothers. But the dreamer in her thought somehow she might just be sitting there watching the swans go by, and suddenly Sarah would appear, and they'd recognize one another instantly and fall into each other's arms.

Edie finally got around to telling Aunt Flo. Aunt Flo didn't seem too surprised, but she wasn't much help either. She didn't remember the name of the agency, she wasn't sure it had been an agency. All she remembered was the two people who'd brought the papers. The man had been a lawyer, he said, the woman a social worker. She couldn't remember their names at all. Edie was disappointed but not that surprised. As she wandered around Boston, she tried to figure out how to get started.

She dropped into a couple of lesbian bars—pretty different from the early days. Both were filled with young women, one with college types and the other, like Rosie's, with a lot of put-on punk.

One night when Edie had had enough of watching affluent young women either being affluent or playing at not being affluent, she found herself driving around Somerville. Waiting at a stoplight, she heard an up-beat *A-Train* coming out an open door. She pulled into a parking space and ducked into a neon-lit barroom with formica tables. A small platform at the side of the room held an upright piano that was being cajoled into performing way beyond its out-of-tune capacity. A tall rawboned woman with a head full of pepper-and-salt curls bent over the keys as if she were literally breathing life into the ivories. She was good. So was the rest of the band—all women. Edie settled onto a barstool and let herself sink into the music. The pianist came out of her solo to the lethargic applause of the half dozen drinkers at the bar, and a short black woman took up the changes on the vibraphone. They all had to be oblivious to the audience to be playing like that—just tossing the energy around amongst themselves.

By the time they finished the set, they'd noticed that

Edie was the only one listening, and they asked her to join them for the break. It was their last gig together, they told her, each of them was about to go their separate ways. The bass player was joining a women's group in California, the drummer was going to the Northeast Kingdom get her head together, the vibraphonist had hooked up with a mixed group here in Boston. And the pianist—Anabelle was her name—was going to Washington.

"To play?" Edie asked.

Anabelle looked at Edie with dark intense eyes. Her long fingers drummed a rhythm on the formica table top.

"Well, I got a gig on Georgia Avenue, but I'm really going so I can find out who I am." She grinned at Edie's puzzled look and continued. "Hey, I'm adopted. I just spent the last six years of my life trying to track down my birth mother, and last month I made it to the last round— got a court order to unlock the agency records. Damned agency's fought me every inch of the way, but I got 'em now. They think adoptees don't need to know anything about themselves before adoption, not even the hour they were born. Now how the hell you gonna have your chart done if you don't even know the hour you were born?"

The woman snorted. Her dark eyes flashed anger, yet her mouth was shaped into a grin that pushed wrinkles onto her broad nose. Her whole body seemed to be in motion as she talked.

Edie was fascinated. "How'd you ever get started?" she asked.

"There's a group at the Women's Center," Anabelle answered. "They call it an adoptees' support group, meets once a month. It's mainly for women who want to find their birth mothers, although sometimes women who have adopted daughters come, too. Why, are you adopted?"

Edie looked away. She had told her story, or at least a shortened version of it several times since that night at Rosie's. Each time she told it, she experienced a sense of dislocation that made her abbreviate it even more.

"I had a daughter I gave up for adoption," she told Anabelle. "I wanted to look for her, but I don't know exactly how to start."

"Why don't you come to the support group? There's a meeting tomorrow night." Anabelle's smile radiated warmth. "I'll be there. It starts at seven-thirty. Oops, time to beat the ivories again. Stay for the second set." She brushed Edie's shoulder lightly as she stood up.

While the band played, Edie watched Anabelle's large hands move gracefully and powerfully over the keyboard. Nice bass line, thought Edie. Nice rhythms, too. She chuckled when she heard Anabelle punctuating a riff with funny sounds that exploded through her full half-open lips.

Edie closed up the bar with them and helped them carry the instruments out to a van. While the drummer wedged the last cymbal in between the snare and the bass, Anabelle hung her arm loosely over Edie's shoulder and repeated the directions to the Women's Center.

"Seven-thirty sharp," she said. "This group starts on time. Be there, okay?"

Edie looked up. Anabelle's eyes were intense, but her smile was warm.

"Okay," she mumbled and stood watching as Anabelle climbed into the van and drove away.

At the Women's Center, Edie was directed to a room where nine women were sitting around on Salvation Army style chairs and sofas. She sat down in a straight-backed chair next to the door and waited. A lanky woman

42

in a red plaid shirt looked at her watch and said, "Let's get started," introduced herself as Nina and suggested that they check in around the circle with just names. She said that then those who wanted to could tell about their searches and those who weren't ready could take their time. Edie relaxed when she realized that she wouldn't be put on the spot and settled back to listen to Nina's story.

"I only found out I was adopted," the woman began, "when I was in the hospital ten years ago. They told me that my blood type couldn't have come out of my parents' blood types. When I confronted them, they reacted by being hurt that I'd want to look for my birth mother. I put it off for a few years, but eventually I had to come back to it. It kept nagging me. I finally found out the name of the town I was born in from one of my mother's sisters. I passed myself off as a reporter and sneaked into the town records—just like a TV show. My original birth certificate was still there, right beside the amended certificate, someone had forgotten to seal it. "

"So your search was over?" asked one of the younger women.

"My search was just beginning. The original birth certificate told me my birth mother's name and the hospital I was born in, which was in upstate New York. The hospital, of course, dismissed me quickly when I tried to get any more information. My birth mother's name was Louisa Cooke, so I picked up the phone book and called every Cooke in the county. When I'd exhausted that county, I started with the next one over. I made a map of the whole state and just worked my way methodically through one county after another. I checked the telephone directories, the voter registration lists and the motor vehicle registrations for a period of about five years either side of my birth. I finally located a cousin who admitted to knowing about the scandal, as she called it. She'd lost track of my mother years ago, everybody in the family had. But she gave me a couple of clues which led to a couple more." The woman paused, a little out of breath. The room was still as a pin, everyone waiting for the story to go on.

"Oh, you don't need to know every detail. I spent seven years tracking her down. She'd changed her name three times and lived all over the country. I finally located her, with her latest husband, living in the Connecticut. And then, after all that searching, I lost my nerve. I waited six months before I finally wrote her a letter, telling her who I was, what I was doing with my life, where I was living. And gave her my phone number. Then I waited. Every time the phone rang, I jumped, and my hands started sweating. About two weeks after I mailed the letter, she called. When I answered, she said, in an absolutely neutral voice, 'This is the person you wrote the letter to.' I was a basket case. Then she started to warm up a bit, and we talked for an hour. We've talked on the phone four or five times now. I'm planning to drive down there next week to meet her for the first time. I guess I'm looking for a little support to help me over this final hurdle."

Edie listened, as fascinated as the rest. It was the first time Edie'd gotten a sense of what the mechanics of a search might involve. It seemed overwhelming.

A woman with a tight worn smile spoke next.

"My search wasn't nearly so hard as yours. I always knew my birth mother's name because someone at the hospital had left my little ID bracelet on. I just sent off my two dollars and asked for my birth certificate. It turned out that my parents were married when I was born and were still married when I found them in the New Haven city directory. I go down and see my mother every couple of months, but my father won't see me. My mother says he considers me to be dead. It's hard for my mother. She wants to see me, but she has to do it secretly. She's been under his thumb for so long, she doesn't dare go against his wishes."

The woman's smile faded.

"But it sounds like she is daring to go against his wishes," someone said. "Even if she has to do it secretly. Maybe knowing you will give her the courage she needs to be her own self."

"That's what I tell myself every time I go. But it's still hard. I find I'm really angry with her sometimes—I just want to shake her and make her see that she doesn't need to follow his every order. But she's been that way for so long—I don't really know if I'm helping her or making her life more miserable."

Edie wondered what she would do if she found Sarah in an impossible marriage. Even though she knew Sarah was thirty-two years old, she really still saw her as a four-month-old infant. If she tried real hard, she could project an eight- or nine-year-old skinny frame onto her. Beyond that she couldn't imagine.

She pulled out of her thoughts to hear one of the younger women say she hadn't started her search yet, she was trying to find the courage. When the woman with the tight smile asked her why, what was she afraid of, the younger woman started talking about her feelings of fear and confusion. Several other women joined in and started to describe their feelings. Edie began to fidget. Feelings talk always bored her. It seemed to her that a lot of women spent so much time trying to figure out how they felt that they never got around to actually feeling anything.

Her attention wandered. She examined the room in

detail. In addition to the overstuffed chairs and sofas, there was a small round table with a large table lamp with a Chinese dragon on it. Next to that, a floor-to-ceiling bookcase was filled with books. It was handmade out of pine, and Edie noticed that whoever had made it hadn't used nails—it was held together with dowels. Nice work. Her eyes were lingering over a couple of interesting book titles when the buzz of voices separated itself into words.

"I think I'm afraid to find my mother because I'm really pretty angry with her. I mean, why didn't she keep me? Why'd she give me away? Lots of women raise kids alone, who needs a husband to help out, they don't help out anyway."

Another woman joined in. "Yeah, I feel like that, too. I think my mother really copped out. Sure, it wouldn't have been easy, but being adopted wasn't easy either. I feel so rejected."

Edie felt herself getting hot under the collar. She didn't know why, but what the women said really pissed her. When she heard herself say "shit" under her breath, she knew it was time to leave. She got up, jerked open the door, walked through it and let it slam behind her. She bumped into somebody in the hall and started to shove on past her. A strong hand gripped her shoulder.

"Hey there, where you going in such a rush? The meeting can't be over, I'm not that late."

It was Anabelle. Edie turned and Anabelle said, "Uh-oh, looks like somebody said something you didn't like."

Edie stared at her, still boiling, ready to tell her to go to hell. "You're goddamn right somebody said something. Those goddamn little twits, what the hell do they know? They're in there pissing and moaning, they're angry at their mothers, for godsakes, they feel rejected, the little assholes. Why don't they get angry at the people who took them away from their mothers? Why don't they...."

"Whoa back a minute," said Anabelle. "You lost me. Slow down a bit."

Edie told her what the women had said and added that she'd really had enough of listening to babyfart self-pity.

"So you're gonna just leave? You're gonna let them say that and walk out?"

"I'm gonna go get me a double shot of Jack Daniels, take my mind off this crap."

"Oh, no, you're not, not yet. You're gonna turn right around and go back in there with me and give them a little education."

Anabelle didn't give her any choice. She put one arm around her shoulder while the other hand gripped her elbow and marched her right through the door without knocking. The room fell silent.

"My friend Edie's a little upset about something some of you said, and I think we need to talk about it."

Nobody said anything. The two young women looked a little worried.

"Go on, Edie. Tell them how you feel."

Edie felt stupid. She was still mad, but she didn't know what to say.

"Have a seat, both of you, before you lay it on us." The words from Nina, the woman who'd spoken first, broke the tension in the room.

Anabelle and Edie sat down. Edie looked for the right words. She started out talking slowly to keep her voice calm.

"How do you know that your mothers *wanted* to give you up? How do you know that they had any choice in the matter? You don't know anything at all about your mothers and what was happening in their lives when they had you. Maybe they gave you up so they could

47

party. But maybe you got adopted because they didn't have any say in the matter."

She stopped. The whole room was watching her. She took a deep breath and plunged on.

"I had my daughter jerked right out of my arms. I was holding her, I was taking care of her, I was doing okay. And they came right to my room and took her away. They said I wasn't moral enough to bring her up. And it wasn't because I fucked one boy one time—I could've fucked him a hundred times and it'd've been okay if I'd've married him. I got away from my parents, I got away from the goddamn nuns, I got away from my Aunt Flo. But they still got me. Came right to my room and took her out of my arms, carried her off screaming and yelling...."

Edie choked on the words and stopped. Anabelle kept her arm tight around her shoulders and started to talk quietly.

"She's not the only mother in the world who got a kid yanked out of her arms. I taught piano in an Indian Center once in Vancouver. Do you have any idea how many of those men and women didn't grow up with their parents? Got carted off to a church-run boarding school two provinces away and didn't see their families for years? Even now, in this country, a lot of Indians end up in court listening to some social worker testifying that they drink too much or fuck too much or are just too damn Indian and, zap, their kids are in foster care or a-dopted by some white family."

There was a long silence in the room. Then a woman spoke up and told how she had quit being a social worker because one of her jobs was to declare mothers unfit.

"And, yes," she said, "some of the women were unfit to be mothers. Some of them were junkies and would have let their kids starve for a nickel bag. But a lot of them were just women without any money. They'd get arrested for shoplifting or passing bad checks or helping a boyfriend deal drugs. And while they were in prison, the state would take over their kids. I was part of the process. I was just out of school with an MSW. I had the usual middle-class attitude toward women in prison, I was perfect for the job of convincing them their kids were better off away from them. At first I really believed it. Then I finally started listening to the women—not to mention the kids—and I realized I couldn't take it. I quit the job and I quit the profession."

Edie was all ears. What had happened to her had happened to a lot of women. Apparently it wasn't uncommon for some woman to be branded as unfit for motherhood and lose her child to the people who branded her. She could sense that what she had said herself had touched off some charge of energy. The room was filled with voices as different women told stories—their own or ones they'd heard. It took Edie a while to realize that what she was listening to was politics. Each of the stories—whether about obstacles thrown up in the adoption search or about losing children to higher authorities—fit into a pattern that fit Edie's own experience. She liked the way these women looked at the world. She'd never had much time for the women-are-oppressed talk she'd heard at Rosie's. The women who talked it never seemed too oppressed to her with their husky private school voices and the interest from Daddy's trust in their hip pockets. But when these women talked about changing the system, their talk made sense. They were making things happen—first by doing it themselves and then by telling others.

Everybody was fired up. When a woman came in and announced that the Center was closing, nobody wanted to leave. They lingered, talking in small groups. Anabelle squeezed Edie's elbow.

"Glad you came back?" She smiled.

"Yeah, I owe you for that," Edie responded.

"I forgot to ask you last night—did you check the hospital she was born in? Sometimes you can find somebody cooperative there."

Edie frowned. "I didn't have her in a hospital," she said. "Jesus, I just realized I didn't even get a birth certificate for her. I had her in this rented room I was living in. My Lithuanian landlady helped me deliver. God, I was so dumb, I didn't even think about registering the birth. I guess my landlady didn't think about it either."

"Hey, so what, you were just a kid. Let's see, you mentioned nuns," said Anabelle. "Was the agency part of the church?"

"Dunno," said Edie. "Aunt Flo never was religious that I knew of, but she might have gone through the church. I can ask her."

"Well, if it was, the Catholic Church is one tough nut to crack. They keep all kinds of records, but they usually won't let anybody see them. Give it a try. You don't have anything to lose. Anyway, you gotta start somewhere. Good luck."

Anabelle reached out and ruffled Edie's hair. Then she turned and strode off down the street. Edie looked after her. She was right. Edie climbed into her truck and turned the ignition. She was ready to roll.

Edie fixed Aunt Flo her favorite meal—corned beef, cabbage and potatoes—and let her finish it before she brought up the subject. She still wasn't all that comfortable talking with her about it. Aunt Flo didn't seem to disapprove of the search, but still she was reserved. The two of them talked about this and that while they ate. Then, after the plates were pushed back and Aunt Flo had lit her cigarette, Edie asked her how she found the people that placed Sarah. Aunt Flo's face clouded over. She looked down at the tablecloth.

"Well, Edie, I didn't exactly find the people, they found me. I really didn't know what to do when you showed up on my doorstep. I always felt pretty special about you. Showing up pregnant was about the last thing I would have expected from you. I called your mother, of course, but when I said I wouldn't send you back to the Home, she said she'd never speak to either of us again and hung up. I really didn't know what to do. I didn't earn enough to pay a hospital bill, I didn't see how you could possibly keep the baby. You hadn't even finished high school, you were just a kid yourself.

"So I told Charlene about it. She advised me to tell Father McCreary, the priest over in South Boston where we grew up. I hadn't been to mass or confession since I'd left home and didn't want to have anything to do with the Church. But Charlene pointed out that finding homes for unwanted babies was something the Church was very good at, that the hospital bills would be paid, and the child would have a good solid home. I kept putting it off, and you kept getting bigger and bigger. In the end, Charlene was the one who went, not to the priest but to one of the sisters at one of the parochial schools here in Charlestown, someone who was the cousin of a friend of hers. Then soon after that, those two people came to the house and introduced themselves as a lawyer and a social worker who were in charge of finding homes for unwanted children. They said they already had a young couple waiting, very good people, he had a well paying job, they lived in a good neighborhood."

"So it wasn't an agency after all, it was part of the Church?"

"Well, now that you ask me, I'm not sure. I don't know that they even called it an agency. When they said lawyer and social worker, I assumed it was an agency. I didn't really think about it. I was just so relieved that the problem would be solved, that the baby would find a home. It wasn't like it is now, with not enough babies to go around to couples who want to adopt. In those days, a child could spend months, even years in an orphanage. And once a child was past five, there wouldn't be much hope of it ever being adopted. It seemed very fortunate to me that your baby was going to have a home right away."

"Think, Aunt Flo," urged Edie. "Did they mention a church? Or any name at all?"

Aunt Flo closed her eyes and sat very still, her hands wrapped around her coffee cup. Edie held her breath and listened to the clock ticking. Finally Aunt Flo spoke.

"Heavenly Rest. The Church of the Heavenly Rest," she said slowly. "How could I have forgotten, the name was so apt."

"Is there a Church of the Heavenly Rest here in Charlestown?" asked Edie.

"Lord, Edie, I wouldn't know. If I hadn't been to mass in years then, how long do you think it is now?"

"Well, they must be listed in the phone book. Here, let's have a look." She picked up the telephone book and started to flip through the Cs. "Church of Christ, sixteen of them at least, Church of Jesus Christ, LDS, oops, I went too far. Here it is. Church of the Heavenly Rest. No, it's not in Charlestown, it's in Medford. Not too far from here, though, I guess it must be the one. I'll check it out. What about the nun Charlene talked to? Do you remember her name, the name of the school?"

"Oh, Edie, it's been thirty-two years." Aunt Flo ran her fingers along the edge of the oilcloth.

"What else do you remember?" persisted Edie. "The name of the lawyer, the social worker? Where did they go after they took Sarah?"

Aunt Flo got up and poured herself another cup of coffee. When she sat down again, she put both hands around the cup and held on to it.

"You know, Edie, right up until that moment in that room in Watertown, I thought I was doing the right thing. I never considered any other possibility. That lawyer and social worker seemed quite decent. And I was really angry with you. I paid back the money you stole from the nuns, and then you stole money from me. Our family didn't do things like that. And I just didn't understand why you were doing what you were doing. It didn't seem right, not for the child's sake or for yours.

"So when I took them there, I was in a real peak. I really

believed you were doing the wrong thing. Then they came in, and their whole manner seemed different from the way they'd been before. When they took that child out of your arms, something in me said that it wasn't right. I followed them out to the car, and I asked them didn't they think they should go back and get some of the baby's things, at least. Everything was happening so fast, I couldn't figure out what was wrong. And your baby was just screaming, I couldn't think. But their whole manner toward me changed as soon as they had that baby in their hands. It was like I didn't exist any more. The man was really brusque and told me to get in the back seat of the car. They dropped me off at a bus stop without a word. I realized the child was sick, and they wanted to get it to a doctor. But still, I guess I felt that the way they acted wasn't right, and I didn't know what to do about it. So I put it out of my mind, just put it clean out of my mind. When you turned up a couple of years later on your motorcycle, it seemed like a closed chapter."

"Well, it was until I opened it." Edie leaned back in her chair. "I don't think it's going to be easy to get any information out of the church, but I'll check it out in the morning. Maybe if you keep it in the back of your mind, you'll remember something else."

On her way to the Church of the Heavenly Rest, Edie remembered the woman's story from the night before, the one who had passed herself off as a reporter. She knew she couldn't just ask a priest to help her find her illegitimate child, but could she pull off any kind of impersonation? She didn't know how reporters talked, except from TV. And what was she even looking for? What kind of records did the church keep, anyway?

The church, when she found it, was unimpressive. The

rectory garden was weeded over, and one of the stained glass windows was taped where a stone had been thrown through it. Edie rang the bell hanging by the door of the rectory and waited. When no one answered, she pulled the bell rope again. Just as she was turning to go away, the door creaked open. She turned back to find an incredibly wizened and bent over woman in black staring at her.

"I want to see some church records," she said, not knowing how much to say to her and how much to wait for the priest for. The housekeeper just stared without a glimmer of comprehension. Edie repeated her request. The woman turned and disappeared into the house. The door stayed open, so Edie guessed she was supposed to wait on the step.

After what seemed like a very long time, the woman returned and motioned Edie to follow her. Inside, the house was dark and dingy. The wallpaper had columns of grimy flowers, the drapes were dark and purply and unevenly hung. As they passed through the front room, Edie noticed a coal stove and the smell of damp coal dust. It was the smell of the soft coal her family had burned when she was kid, she didn't know anybody burned that anymore. Or maybe the smell was just there from twenty years ago.

The housekeeper opened a heavy door and stood back to let Edie pass into the priest's study. Then she withdrew, closing the door behind her. The room was so dark, Edie couldn't see anyone at first. Then a figure even more wizened and bent over than the housekeeper came into focus. He was behind a great mahogany desk with piles of papers on it. He looked at Edie but didn't say anything.

"I'm looking for some records," Edie started, not sure how to proceed. "Of a child that was born in this church in 1955." Looking at him, Edie decided she might pass herself off as a lawyer for a rich aunt.

He didn't say anything, so she went on.

"I represent the estate of Millicent MacIntire. Her will states that her estate is to be divided amongst her nieces and nephews, one of which was born in this church." Edie felt like she was blundering. How did she know how inheritances got divided. But this bird didn't look like he knew either, so she continued.

"I only know her first name as Sarah and that she was born sometime in January of 1955. So if you have records of births from that time, I'd like to see them." Edie stopped, not knowing how to go on. The priest was still staring at her. Finally he spoke, his head tilting slightly to one side and his speech a little slurred.

"The records. Gone. All gone. They took them away. There. See that empty space? There by the door? A file cabinet was there. After the break-in, they said it wasn't safe to keep records here. The locks weren't good enough. They came with a truck. The monsignor sent them, they said. Two men with a truck. They carried them out, file cabinet and all. They took them all away. But it wasn't the monsignor, I asked him. He said he didn't have my file cabinet. Or my papers. But the papers were gone before. The papers have been gone for years. No one's born here anymore anyway. No one's baptized. They're all gone."

His voice trailed off. Edie realized it didn't make any difference whether she passed herself off as a lawyer or a coathanger. He didn't even seem to notice as she walked out, he just kept nodding his head and saying, "Gone, all gone." Edie got out as fast as she could, waving the housekeeper aside as she tried to open the front door. Outside, she found herself almost in tears. What a dope. That's what you get, Edie, old girl. Pick a church out of the phone book and like as not find a loony.

Edie spent the rest of the day in a little bar across from an auto repair shop in Medford. Dead ended at the church. What next. She finally wandered back to the apartment in the late evening. Aunt Flo was asleep in her arm chair, her book fallen onto the floor. She woke with a start as Edie came in.

"Oh, Edie! You startled me. I've been waiting for you. Did you find out anything at the church?"

"Just a decaying old priest who lost his records along with his marbles years ago. Sorry I'm late, I needed a little fortification."

"Well, I did better than you then." Aunt Flo said brightly. "I remembered the lawyer's name. Harold Grafton. All last night I kept waking up trying to remember the social worker's name, because she was the one I talked to the most. And I never liked him. He was officious, and I don't trust lawyers anyway. But this morning it was his name that came to me. Harold Grafton. I thought there must be somewhere where lawyers are listed."

Edie stared at her.

"You mean that hatchet face who came to Watertown? The lawyer? You remembered his name?"

"Yes! It came to me this morning in a flash. I asked Marge at the office where I could find a list of lawyers. And she got her granddaughter who's a lawyer on the phone. So we went over there to her office at lunch, and she brought out this big book that lists every lawyer in the country. And sure enough, there he was, Harold Grafton. He works for...here, I have it here somewhere..." Aunt Flo fumbled in her apron pocket and drew out a slip of paper. "...he works for Tippet, Fox, Everly, Grafton and Brown. On Boylston Street. But that's not all. Marge's granddaughter dug out the list they published in 1955. And listen to this, he wasn't listed there. Edie, that man wasn't a lawyer when you signed those papers. He lied to me. He wasn't a lawyer at all then. Maybe the woman wasn't a social worker."

Edie stared at her. "Aunt Flo, what kind of papers did I sign, anyway? I never read them, everybody was just telling me to sign."

"Oh, Lord, Edie, I didn't read them myself. They looked official, I can't read legal things. I just signed like you did, wherever they told me to. I wasn't even your legal guardian, I should have known something wasn't right."

"No use crying over it now." The pencil in Edie's hand had traced the name Harold Grafton over and over on the phone pad until the letters were all a scribble. Then she took the slip of paper from Aunt Flo and looked at it.

"What are you going to do?" asked Aunt Flo.

"I'm going to call him. I'm going to make him tell me what he did with my daughter."

Edie looked at the wall clock. It was almost eleven. Too late to call tonight. Tomorrow was Thursday, she'd call then. She couldn't believe it, the man was still right here in town, still grabbing babies for all she knew. No, now he was a real lawyer with a high-rent address, he'd moved up in the world. He was probably stealing railroads now.

Edie woke up at six A.M., her stomach clutching. The Church of the Heavenly Rest had been just a warm-up. This was the real thing. This was the man who had had her sign papers, this was the hatchet face who'd torn Sarah out of her arms. Angry as she was, her mind was clear. Tuesday night she had connected her own loss with the losses of other women who, like her, had been doing the best they could. Not great by other people's standards maybe, but all right considering the odds. This Grafton character was probably no different from a million other jerks who thought they were acting in the best interests of other people when in reality they always acted in the best interests of themselves. If people couldn't be made to do what they wanted done smoothly with paperwork, the Graftons of the world would march in and do it violently and still have self-righteous written all over their faces.

Edie rolled off the couch and started to dress. To hell with telephoning, she thought, I'll go straight to the bastard's office and confront him in person. She ironed a fresh crease in her khakis and pulled on her best tweed jacket.

At ten o'clock, she stood in front of the Waymore Building, thirty stories of glass and steel, a thousand offices stacked on top of each other, a million pieces of paper being filed every minute. Let's get on with it, she thought. Her anger propelled her past the doorman and lobby receptionists and onto the elevator. At the eleventh floor, the door opened directly into a wood paneled reception area.

"Do you have an appointment?" A blue-eyed manikin smiled at her from behind an imitation walnut desk.

"No, I'm here to reclaim some papers I signed thirty-two years ago with your Mr. Grafton. I'd like to see him right away."

The receptionist eyed Edie's khakis with doubt and rang the inner recesses.

"Sue? There's a woman out here who wants to see Mr. Grafton about an old case. Do you want to handle it?"

She turned to Edie.

"What did you say your name was?"

"Edie Cafferty. The papers were signed in 1955. They

were for an adoption."

"She says her name is Cafferty, Edie Cafferty," she repeated into the phone. "It's about a 1955 adoption case."

The woman listened for a moment and then hung up the phone.

"I'm sorry, but Mr. Grafton's secretary is busy today. If you'd care to make an appointment, I can fit you in early next week."

"Actually I don't want to see Mr. Grafton's secretary. I want to see Mr. Grafton himself. And I think he'll want to see me. The papers were signed illegally, he wasn't even a lawyer then, and I was underage. He can either see me, or I can file a complaint with the bar association. Take your pick."

A slight frown creased the receptionist's brow. She picked up the phone reluctantly.

"Sue? I'm sorry to bother you again, but Miss Cafferty has some information that I think you'll have to handle...."

Edie plucked the telephone out of her hands.

"Sue? This is Edie Cafferty. You tell your boss that I'll give him fifteen minutes to let me in his office before I start tearing down the door. He impersonated a lawyer before he was one, and I'm here to tell whoever's interested if he can't manage to see me."

She slammed down the phone and waited. A few seconds later the panel door opened, and a willowy brunette in mauve ushered Edie through it. Annoyance barely showed in her lacquered face as she indicated a plush chair for Edie to sit in.

"Mr. Grafton is with a client right now. If you'll give me your name again and the date of the case, I'll see what I can do."

She poised her Cross pen.

"Edie Cafferty." Edie spoke slowly, carving each word. "January 1955. The papers were actually signed in August of 'fifty-four, but the child was born in 'fifty-five. Mr. Grafton wasn't a lawyer until 1958. I'm not interested in filing a complaint unless Mr. Grafton isn't interested in seeing me. Tell him."

The young woman impassively jotted notes on her pad and then slipped through the door behind her desk. Edie looked around the room. Wood panelling back here, too. The desk was six feet long with a carefully positioned desk organizer at one end and an ivory telephone at the other. A computer terminal glowed a familiar spread sheet. Fancy surroundings, thought Edie, but she probably does the same kind of work I did.

The door opened, and Mr. Grafton appeared. He was gray, all gray—gray suit, gray eyes, gray hair, gray face. Edie stood up, her anger strong but under control.

"Miss Cafferty? Will you step this way, please?"

This place was a set of Chinese boxes, each more elegant than the last. The desk here was at least ten feet long, the carpet two inches thicker. Mr Grafton closed the door behind them.

"I understand you're looking for some papers you say you signed in 1954. I'm afraid my records don't go back that far. Perhaps you can refresh my memory. I've had thousands of cases in my career."

"Quit bluffing, mac. You're running scared, or you wouldn't have seen me. The case was an adoption. You passed yourself off as a lawyer to my aunt, Florence Cafferty. Fortunately for you, I'm not interested in your ethics. I just want information about my daughter. Who adopted her?"

"Oh, my goodness, I couldn't give you that information, even if I had it. As I said, I have no records for then. But even if I did, you'd have to get a court order to unseal them. That's the law. But anyway, I simply don't have the information you're seeking. Surely you don't expect me to remember something that happened in 1954, 1955."

"Maybe you haven't gotten the picture yet, Grafton. You committed a crime when you ripped that kid out of my arms. You had me sign papers I couldn't legally sign because I was only sixteen. And you weren't even a lawyer."

"My dear Miss Cafferty. Where are these alleged papers? You don't have them, I don't have them. Maybe they exist only in your mind. You and your aunt are operating under a cloak of misinformation. It's quite true that I wasn't a lawyer in 1954. Neither did I impersonate one. I held a position of some authority with the church. I was what would be called a deacon nowaday, and as such I was empowered by the church to assist in placing unfortunates with families who could care for them. If you and your aunt thought I was a lawyer, it's an understandable mistake, but I assure you that I did not ever present myself as one."

The oily voice began to take on a steel edge.

"Whatever papers you signed, Miss Cafferty, you signed legally because your aunt signed them with you. If she passed herself off as your legal guardian when she wasn't, then it is she who has committed the crime, not I. Of course, it was only a little crime, and I wouldn't want to take on the prosecution of it, even my friends on the bench would think it not worth the court's time...."

Edie's mind exploded. The bastard remembered the case, he remembered that Aunt Flo had signed the papers, she hadn't said anything about that. And his smooth lawyer talk was twisting the facts, turning them upside down. He was rattling his power at her, too, reminding her that the justice-for-all club is run by men just like himself.

"You son of a bitch, you know exactly what I'm talking about. You think a posh office and friends who are judges puts you above the law? You think being a so-called deacon of the church gives you the right to take babies from mothers you don't approve of and give them to the ones you do? You lied to my aunt, you stole my daughter, you left me with no way to ever see her again. I may've had only a basement room in a cold water flat, but it was my life. You and your goddamn morals. You broke the law, you bastard. If you don't know who adopted her, you better tell me who does. I'm not afraid of you and your goddamn judge friends, I'll take this case to the Supreme Court, I'll...."

"Miss Cafferty, Miss Cafferty, please calm down."

The door opened.

"It's all right, Sue, she's just a little upset. I can handle it." He turned back to Edie. "Now Miss Cafferty, I do understand your distress. And I believe I can help you some. At that time I was in the Church of the Heavenly Rest parish. It's not much of a parish anymore, I believe it's been a little neglected. But I expect they still have a priest. You should go see him, perhaps the records are there."

The strength that had been carrying Edie along suddenly broke as Edie realized the truth in what the lawyer was saying. She could file a hundred complaints, but it wouldn't get her the information she needed to find Sarah. Afraid that her voice would show her defeat, she turned and walked out, past the secretary, past the receptionist. Out on the street, she ducked into the first bar and ordered a beer. Goddamn, they could stack the cards against people. When her beer came, she downed it in one gulp

63

and ordered another one. Then she caught a glimpse of herself in the mirror behind the bar. A woman was staring back at her with reddish brown hair and steel blue eyes. The eyes were angry, but they were still clear. Come on, Edie, she thought to herself. This is the second time in two days you've run for the bar. That woman last night spent years tracking her mother down. She must have had hundreds of dead ends. This is just a few days out. There are a lot more ways to look for Sarah.

She dug her hands in her pockets and felt a wad of paper. It was a cocktail napkin from the bar Anabelle had played at. On the corner was her phone number. Edie pictured her broad face with the full smile and walked over to the phone booth. She dialed the number, let it ring ten times and was about to hang up when Anabelle picked up the phone, breathless. Edie asked her if she was still going to Washington.

"Sure am," she said, breathing hard. "I was just doing some last minute errands so I can get myself onto the midnight train."

"What would you say to going down tomorrow morning in my truck?" Edie asked her. She hadn't thought of it until the words were out of her mouth. But she suddenly wanted to be with Anabelle and tell her what had happened.

"Sounds great. I never can sleep on the train anyway."

Anabelle gave directions to the house she was staying at in Jamaica Plain. Edie told her she'd pick her up around eight. She didn't have any idea what she would do in Washington, but everything here seemed like a dead end. Maybe there were records of some kind in Washington, social security, birth records, whatever. Maybe Anabelle could give her some tips on where to look. Anyway, the trip would give her a breather while she regrouped her forces.

Early the next morning, the two women hit the Mass Turnpike singing. Anabelle's voice was clear and high as she sang one pop tune after another. At first Edie was shy to join in, but Anabelle kept prodding her, and finally Edie let her low bathtub growl make its way into the melodies. They sang all the way to Hartford where they stopped for coffee.

"I haven't sung like that since I was eleven," said Anabelle. "Damn, I forgot how good it feels."

"I never sang like that before," Edie told her. "If I'd known it was that kind of high—it's almost as good as sex."

"Better," said Anabelle, "you don't get sweaty."

The Howard Johnson waitress raised an eyebrow as she set down the coffees.

"When I was eleven..." Anabelle settled back in the red plastic covered seat and let her eyes focus in the distance. "When I was eleven, my parents brought a girl out from Roxbury to spend the summer. See, my father was a business man, and his politics were garden variety conservative. But my mother was an all-men-are-brothers YWCA-er. She really believed that if only people of different races could know each other, there'd be no more wars, no more poverty, no more problems in the world. She was a real enigma because politically she voted Republican with my father, but socially she had this integrationist attitude. This is before Brown versus Board of Education, right?" Anabelle's long finger poked the air. "And she's in Boston every Tuesday and Thursday afternoon, volunteering at the Y, leading discussion groups with teenagers. My father went along with it because he saw the social world as her sphere of influence. He didn't care what she did so long as she didn't overshoot the household budget and try to spend more money than he carefully doled out every Monday morning."

Anabelle punctuated the sentence by dropping imaginary pennies into her by now empty coffee cup.

"Anyway, my mother had met this woman at the Y, one of the switchboard operators. She had helped her fill out scholarship forms for her son who wanted to go to Northeastern to be an engineer. When she found out the woman had a daughter my age, she invited her to spend the summer with me."

Anabelle paused as the waitress refilled their cups.

"So Mattie arrived the week after school let out," she continued, "and we started singing the very first day. She taught me a style of singing I'd never heard before—early Motown—and we'd harmonize from the time we got up 'til the time we went to bed. Then she got my parents to drive us back to her house, and she persuaded her brother to loan her some of his records. And then I really got hooked.

"See, my parents were pretty well off, but culture wasn't one of their things. The only pictures on the wall of our house were photographs of me in the first grade, the second grade, the third grade. And the only books on the shelf were the twenty-two volumes of the World

Books. There was an old phonograph in the den. Somebody must've listened to music once upon a time, because there was a handful of Glenn Miller records. Which I thought were just great until Mattie played me her brother's collection. Coltrane, Bird, Lady Day, Sarah Vaughn. I couldn't believe my ears. It was a whole new world to me. We listened for hours at a time. My mother complained that we weren't outside being healthy, so we'd dutifully march out and walk around the streets of Belmont arm in arm trying to scat. Then we'd sneak back in and listen some more. When Mattie played me a Thelonius Monk, that was it. I knew I had to play piano. All those sounds. I didn't have a clue as to how he was making them, but I wanted to make them, too."

Anabelle's long fingers drummed the table top. She closed her eyes, remembering. Then her face broke into a wicked grin.

"One day, we were listening to Billie singing *Let's Do It*. And suddenly Mattie sits up and kisses me right on the mouth. Well, that knocked me over even more than the Monk had. Simultaneously we said, 'Let's do it!' And by god, we did and every day after that, too. Course, one day my mother walked in on us. You better believe that that was the end of that vacation. Mattie was outa there in thirty minutes flat with all her things. Except the Monk record. She gave that to me, and I gave her a purple silk scarf she liked to tie around her head."

Anabelle chuckled. Edie decided that putting her foot through her parents' bedroom window was small potatoes compared to having a hot little affair at age eleven. She waited for Anabelle to continue.

"I didn't talk to my parents for three weeks," Anabelle went on. "They tried to question me, and I heard them talking about social workers and psychiatrists. But I shut myself up in my room and played that Monk record 'til the grooves were gone. I didn't shed a tear. I just took myself into that other world and stayed there. When I came out, all I said to them was, 'I'm going to play the piano.'

"I gotta give them credit. They really tried with me. That was the first time they told me I was adopted. They gave me the old we-chose-you routine. And of course, 'We're doing what we think is right for you.' Which they were, so far as they could see. Anyway, they did get me a piano and a piano teacher. Classical, of course. Playing by ear was lower class. Jazz was beyond the pale."

"Did you ever see Mattie again?" Edie asked her, as they stood at the cash register waiting to pay the check.

"Well, yes, I did. I'm ashamed to say it took me three years to figure out that the reason she'd left the Monk was because her brother's address was on it. So my first year in high school, I was allowed to get around the MTA on my own, and I tracked her down. She wasn't at that address anymore, but the family that was knew where her family'd gone and so did the next one. It didn't take too many knocking on doors to find her. Her and a kid. And were they pretty together. She told me she'd done it just once to get the kid, and now she and her daughter were gonna grow up strong together. She was living with another girl—they coulda been lovers, maybe not. But I tell you, I was jealous as hell, her starting her life already and me still carrying schoolbooks."

Anabelle's life seemed exotic compared to Edie's. Growing up affluent with parents who brought strangers into your life, compared to Edie's working poor family who visited no one but relatives. Being a musician and traveling around compared to Edie's bookkeeping and living in Vermont for twenty-five years. But as the truck rolled down the interstate, Edie found Anabelle down to earth, straightforward and as easy to talk to as anyone she'd ever been with. They traveled in silence for a while, each one watching spring come more and more to life as they progressed south. Coming off the Tappan Zee Bridge, Anabelle turned to Edie.

"So how'd you get hooked on jazz?" she asked. "I wouldn't've thought there'd be many jazz fans in Vermont."

"Well, you look at White River today," said Edie, "and it's just another bypassed railroad town—empty store fronts, a coupla diners and a department store that hasn't changed its stock since the fifties. When I was growing up, though, it was still in its heyday as a railroad junction. There were two grand hotels on the village square and a whore house over the Greek restaurant. All the name bands used to stop there for one-night stands on their way to Montreal. I heard Count Basie and Woodie Herman and Duke Ellington. Anita O'Day and Ella Fitzgerald and a whole raft of real good singers came through, some of 'em famous, some of 'em no one's heard of since. I didn't know the difference—it was all incredible to me."

"Hunh, imagine hearing that kind of music in the sticks," said Anabelle. "I lived in the big city and never heard a live band 'til I was in college. Go on, what else did you listen to?"

Edie screwed up her face trying to remember when she'd first heard jazz. She wasn't used to thinking about her childhood, it wasn't something she'd much talked about before she started this daughter search. Now it seemed every time she turned around, she was trying to dredge up a memory.

"Let's see, when I was ten or eleven, I got this job Saturday mornings cleaning out the barns of a dairy farmer down old Route 5."

She remembered the sweet strong smell of fresh manure, the feel of her young growing muscles as she flicked each forkful onto the manure heap, the suck of mud on her boots as she trudged through the soggy barnyard. Cleaning up after a herd of thirty-seven Jerseys had netted her three dozen eggs for her family and a quarter for herself.

"I'd be finished by about noon, and the farmer's wife would feed me lunch—left-over stew, usually, but it had real meat in it. This woman, her name was Caroline and she was big as a barn. She was usually in the middle of doing five loads of laundry. She'd be standing in the middle of the kitchen floor running sheets and towels through the wringer and singing. I'd spoon my stew in and listen. Her kids were teenagers, so there wasn't all the hollering and confusion that went on at my house—just the thump of the washing machine and this great big voice belting out song after song. It turned out that she'd been a singer with a bunch of no-name bands, and when she stopped in White River for a show one time, she met and married this farmer. When she saw how interested I was, she started playing me records out of her collection of 78s. We used to listen until her husband came in from milking and complained about the noise and why wasn't dinner on. I got so I could fly through that shit shoveling in no time and then spend the rest of the day with her, listening to her scat with the records. She said she was happy as a farmer's wife. She missed the singing but not the traveling and sleeping in flea-bag hotels and having drunks make passes every time she took a break."

Edie could feel again the warmth of that kitchen with its coal stove radiating heat on a cold spring day. Neither she nor Caroline ever said more than two words to each other. Caroline had tried to get Edie to sing once or twice, but Edie had been too shy to set her thin little voice alongside that golden one. She'd learned all the words, though, and had sung them over and over in her head. She realized that singing with Anabelle earlier in the car was the first time she'd ever sung out loud.

"So you graduated from listening to your farmer's wife," said Anabelle, "to listening to real bands playing in the great city of—what'd you say its name was, River City Junction?"

"White River Junction," corrected Edie. "Yeah, by the time I was a teenager, I'd heard a lot of jazz. My sister and I took to sneaking out at night after my parents fell a-sleep. My sister'd go off and screw her boyfriend I guess, but I hung out around the side doors of the lounges drinking in the sounds. Then I'd go over to my singer friend and tell her all about it. Funny thing, much as she loved jazz, she never went to hear it. I guess her farmer husband thought he'd rescued her from a life of sin and didn't want her to fall back into the clutches of evil."

"But you never studied music, you never took piano lessons?"

"My grandmother had a piano in her parlour—it was an old upright with two candlabras on the front. She always talked about how she was going to give it to my mother so my sister and I could have lessons, but she never did. She and my mother had a big fight when I was about eight. They never got along too well after that. I wanted to be in the school band, but you had to have your own instrument, and we didn't ever have the money. I played a borrowed trumpet for about six months—tried hard to make it sound like the stuff I heard. But then the guy who loaned it to me wanted it back, so that was the end of my trumpet playing."

71

Edie had never shared her passion for jazz with anyone since those afternoons with Caroline. When she lived alone, jazz was a special part of her life, but she never talked about it with anyone. When she had a lover, she listened to whatever music her lovers put on. Now, talking with Anabelle about different musicians and different kinds of jazz, Edie could hear the music in her head. When Anabelle described technically what they were doing, Edie got really excited that somebody could translate what you hear into words. Edie didn't know an E-flat ninth from a basketball, but Anabelle was a born teacher. She patiently explained about chords and harmonies and keys.

All the way down the Jersey Turnpike, Anabelle interspersed her mini-lectures on jazz theory with anecdotes about her life as a musician. Unlike Edie's life in which being one person on the job and another person at home or at Rosie's was taken for granted, Anabelle's life seemed to be all of one cloth. Lovers she mentioned were part of her music world—she'd run off to Rio with a Brazilian flute player in her third year at Berklee, she and a bass guitarist had lived together on the Lower East Side and run a summer program for local kids at the Third Street Music School. Right now she was into celibacy, she said, she didn't have the emotional energy for sex. That's what Rosie said, too, thought Edie. Funny to have two celibate friends. Especially funny since, every once in a while, Edie found herself distracted by a flash of physical attraction. But Anabelle wasn't her type at all. Edie liked her women small and good looking, with long hair if possible. Anabelle was almost six feet tall and her broad face was interesting but not what anyone would describe as pretty.

Crossing the Delaware Bridge, Edie asked Anabelle

how long she'd been searching for her birth mother.

"Well, I've been curious for a long time, but I really only got started about six years ago. When my parents died, I found my birth certificate among their things. The amended birth certificate, that is, although there's nothing to distinguish it from any other birth certificate. No mention of my birth mother or even that I'd been adopted. It did tell me the name of the hospital I was born in— Florence Crittenden in Washington, D.C. So I started there. Sent them a polite request for my birth mother's name, innocent that I was. They sent back an equally polite letter saying they couldn't provide me with that information, they could only release that to my mother. As if she'd want to know who she was.

"Then I tried calling them on the phone. There's a story amongst adoptees of a woman who called her birth hospital every day for six years. Regular as clockwork, picked up the phone every morning, dialed the number, asked for her records, thanked them politely when they refused and hung up. The day a new girl came on the line, she got what she wanted. But I couldn't stay cool. I'd be so angry as soon as the other end picked up, I'd start demanding my rights at them. After six calls I couldn't take it any more."

Anabelle grunted and drummed her fingers on the dash.

"So. A lot of people get to see their records just by going in to the Bureau of Vital Statistics and peering over the counter. But Washington's too big for that. They always stood back from the counter and tilted the book away. One clerk finally condescended to give me the name of the agency my parents had adopted me through. So I wrote them. A Mrs. Johnson wrote back. Explaining why I shouldn't be trying to do this. How my adoptive parents would be deeply hurt after all they'd given me. How it would be harmful to me to know the probably sordid details of my past. How my birth mother had her right to privacy, a right they had assured her when she gave me up. The only way she could give me any information at all, she said, was if my birth mother gave her permission. I wrote and told her to get it, and she wrote again to patiently explain that the agency didn't have the resources to undertake any searches." Anabelle snorted.

"So. I finally decided to try the court route. Everybody said it was hopeless. But what else could I do? I couldn't get at my records through the hospital or the Bureau of Vital Statistics or the adoption agency. The first time around—it wasn't too long after Alex Haley's *Roots* was on television—so I just said I was searching out my roots. The judge said he wouldn't—quote, unquote—cater to my idle curiosity. I waited six months, petitioned again, saying this time I was about to be married, and my future in-laws were concerned about any possible heriditary diseases that might be passed on to their grandchildren. My luck, I got the same damn judge who said he wouldn't cater to *their* idle curiosity. I waited a year this time, got a doctor friend to give me a phony medical record saying I was dying of a rare form of leukemia. Got a friend at Fidelity to give me a phony financial statement saying I was worth half a million. By this time I'd made friends with the Court Clerk who was sympathetic, and she made sure I got a different judge. It worked. I pled that I had only a year to live, my parents were dead, I had no other close relatives, and I wanted to leave my half a million to my blood relations. Money talks loud and clear."

Anabelle's laugh was harsh. Edie glanced over and saw that her face was all screwed up.

"So the order came through last month," Anabelle continued. "I called Mrs. Johnson immediately. She's been trying to put me off, but she finally had to give in and give me an appointment for tomorrow morning. And let me tell you I'm nervous. When I started the search, it *was* more or less idle curiosity. I mean, my parents were okay, no better or worse than any other parents. They loved me, they cared for me, they were my parents. But there's always been this missing piece to my life—somebody out there whose blood is the same as mine. Maybe several somebodies, maybe I've got brothers and sisters, a whole raft of relatives. Anyway, now my idle curiosity is burning determination. I'm dying to know who she is."

Edie pondered Anabelle's story. Determination. That's certainly what it takes. The brick walls people keep throwing up are incredible. What's the point, she thought. Two people want to get together after twenty or thirty years, and the whole damn society is out to prevent it. She wondered what other obstacles she was going to have thrown in her path. If she ever figured out what path she was going to take next. Anabelle's cry broke into her thoughts.

"Look, there's the exit for Georgia Avenue. We made it in record time. Let's get this truck on down to Sixteenth Street."

The house Anabelle directed Edie to was an old three-story brick townhouse on the end of a four-house row that sat on a short steep hill right on Sixteenth Street. Anabelle told her to take a right and guided her through a maze of short narrow streets until they finally found a parking place. It took Edie several hitches to ease the truck into the tight spot between two cars that had bright orange scofflaw locks on their front wheels. As Anabelle led her back through the streets, the late afternoon sun warmed their backs. Whole families sat on the stoops of neat brick rowhouses, dandling babies and talking. They found the house again, climbed the steps and rang the bell. The door was opened by a tall, angular young woman who greeted them casually and ushered them into the house.

Edie looked around. The entryway looked into a huge living room with sixteen foot ceilings. Two steps and three white columns separated the living room from the hallway. Great glass chandeliers hung from the ceiling and a five-foot fireplace dominated one wall. Looking out onto Sixteenth Street were two floor-to-ceiling French doors. With all the elegant trappings, the room was shabby with walls badly in need of paint and dingy

drapes that dragged on the scuffed up floor. Anabelle followed her eye and commented,

"Pretty fancy digs, huh? Once upon a time, at least."

"Yeah," agreed the young woman. "Now the rent's
cheap, at least for this neighborhood, so the landlord
figures he doesn't ever need to paint or repair anything."
She turned to Anabelle and said, "You two can share a
bed, I hope. The room you stayed in last time is the only
one that doesn't have several bodies in it. Want to join us
for dinner?"

In the adjoining dining room, which also had a chande-
lier and two more French doors, four other women were
sitting around a large dining room table. Anabelle introduced Edie around, then raised one eyebrow at the tofu
and seaweed dish on the table and said, "Edie and I are
still renegade flesh eaters, I'm afraid. We'll find something on Columbia Road."

The room they were to share was on the third floor. It
was tiny, with a single window opening out onto Sixteenth Street. The only pieces of furniture were an old
school desk and a futon rolled up against the wall. A
yellow cat stared at them impassively.

"Well, I trust we can share the same pad without any
hankypank," said Anabelle. "I wouldn't want to ruin my
reputation, especially with a hayseed!"

Anabelle's eyes laughed over the sharp words. Edie
turned away quickly so Anabelle wouldn't see her
flushed cheeks. She quickly dug into her grip and exchanged her leather jacket for her old grey tweed.

Out on the street again, Anabelle led her back through
the maze of streets until they finally emerged onto
Columbia Road. Edie was bowled over by the sudden
change. The street was broad and treeless and filled with
people and sounds of all kinds. The neighborhoods they

had just walked through were fairly quiet with a few kids playing and adults sitting out and talking. Except for the house they were staying in, the people were mostly black family people. But Columbia Road surged with humanity of all colors. Blacks, Hispanics, Asians, Africans and Middle Easterners all mingled, calling out to one another and yelling at their kids to stay out of the street. Latin music blared out of a record store on one side of the street while Middle Eastern sounds came out of a restaurant on the other side.

"Yeah, it really is a trip, isn't it," said Anabelle, catching her eye. "Just about all kinds here. There's dudes pushing drugs right outside the yuppie townhouses, and illegal aliens running their own kind of sanctuary movements in the slum apartments. This," she pointed to the storefront they were passing, "is an old style intellectual bookstore, and that," she pointed across the street, "is a hotly contested corner for street walkers. And in the middle of it all, you've got these two great big twenty-four-hour supermarkets trying to run each other out of business. That scrawny yellow cat that stared at you came from this Safeway parking lot."

Edie took it all in silently until Anabelle finally steered her up a short flight of stairs and into a dark restaurant that looked more like a bar than a restaurant. The young waitress wore an exotic scarf around her shoulders and spoke with an accent Edie had never heard before. Edie took one look at the menu and said,

"I think you'd better order for me, I can't even read this."

Anabelle laughed and gave an order to the waitress.

"I had no idea there were so many kinds of people in Washington," said Edie. "I mean, I knew there were all those embassies, but I didn't ever think the city had real people, too."

"Well," said Anabelle, "this is a rare neighborhood. Most of this city is pretty segregated still. An enclave of rich whites lives in one small section and the rest of the city is black—slum black, working black, middle class black, professional black. You see a few black faces in the white areas, but even today, no matter how professional they look, they never know when they're gonna get stopped by a cop because some house in their own neighborhood has been burglarized."

"Is that true or are you just making a point?"

"Sure. I had a friend not too long ago, she was married to one of the drummers I played with. She and another friend were standing on a corner in Georgetown, waiting for a cab she'd called from a restaurant. A couple of plainclothes boys pulled up and said to her, 'Where can we find some action?' She was busy talking to her friend, not paying any attention, and just tossed over her shoulder, 'Depends on what kind of action you looking for, mac,' and wham, next thing you know she's handcuffed with her friend in the backseat of the car. Booked 'em both for soliciting, her friend hadn't even opened her mouth."

"But she got off, didn't she?" asked Edie.

"She not only got off, she sued the hell out of the cop who booked her. Unluckily for him, the judge's daughter who was going to Howard looked just like her. I expect that cop thought twice before he pulled another racist stunt like that."

Their food arrived. Edie stared at it. The single large platter took up the entire table. The food was arranged in little piles on a thin piece of baked dough that covered the platter. There was no silverware.

"What kinda food is this, anyway?" asked Edie, frowning at the platter.

"Ethiopian. Don't worry, it won't bite you. The dough is both your plate and your fork," said Anabelle, laughing at Edie's face. "Go on, take a chance, dig in. This is the big city, go with it."

Edie watched her break off a piece of the dough and scoop up a meatball. "I'll try anything once," she muttered, thinking that what she really wanted was a nice steak and a baked potato.

As she ate, Edie had to admit that the food wasn't bad, although eating with her fingers made her uncomfortable. She kept sneaking glances at the other customers to assure herself that it wasn't some kind of Cousin Rube joke. But nobody else had a knife or fork, everyone was indeed using the dough to pick up the other food.

Anabelle was talking about her life in Washington in the sixties when she'd been actively involved in the civil rights movement. Being basically apolitical, Edie had seen the civil rights movement in much the same way she'd seen the Vietnam War. Terrible things were being done to people far away, but it didn't have anything to do with her. She'd never really talked to anybody who'd been involved in either movement. She'd overheard a lot of political talk at Rosie's, but it was always from those same stringy-haired young women who criticized her life style. They seemed to bounce from one set of protests to another, always flaunting their raggeddy-ass clothes and talking about how they didn't have any bread. When their Saabs or Volvos didn't run, of course, they just drove them to the nearest mechanic and had them fixed. Listening to Anabelle, Edie realized that she'd missed the heart of the movement—plain ordinary people saying 'no.'

"The place has changed a lot since then," Anabelle was saying. "It was really just another sleepy southern town.

A lot of people were just one generation away from country. It seemed small and friendly. Now it's mostly people working sixty-hour weeks and eyeing their civil service promotions. But still, it's a comfortable city, I like it here. That is, I feel real at home with the black people here and a little edgy around whites. Don't know why, it's not the same at all in Boston or New York. There, the people I hang out with feel pretty much the same, black or white. But here, especially when I'm playing with these people I've booked in with on Georgia Avenue, I feel real comfortable. They're all men and they all have wives and kids and live in a world nothing like anything I live in. We don't even talk that much. But I play better with them than I play with anyone. And whenever I'm here with them, I feel like I'm home."

Anabelle yawned. Edie looked at the clock on the wall.

"Good God, it's after midnight," she said. "And you're supposed to go see Mrs. Johnson of the Fairview Adoption Agency in the morning and play a gig in the evening. Time for bed."

Anabelle did not see Mrs. Johnson of the Fairview Agency the next day. "'There's been a misunderstanding, I'm afraid,'" she mimicked as she got off the phone. "It seems the board doesn't meet until the end of next week and, court order or no court order, the agency cannot di-vulge the contents of my file until the board approves. Another damn delaying tactic. But, by God, it'll be the last one. Come on, Edie, let's go be tourists."

Driving around Washington was pretty much like driving around Boston, Edie discovered. Traffic was a little slower, but it was still a dodge-'em-cars style of driving. And you damn well better know where you were going and how to get there, she discovered, or you might find yourself crossing a bridge into Virginia. Which she did twice before finding a place to park on Capitol Hill.

Inside the hush of the Capitol building, she and Anabelle threaded their way through knots of high school seniors getting their last lesson in civics. After twenty minutes, she was ready to go. They stood on the steps of the Capitol and watched large groups of teen-agers being herded in one direction or another.

"Isn't the Library of Congress around here somewhere?"

asked Edie.

"Right across the street. You want to go see it?"

"Well, I thought there might be some kind of records they keep there that I could be looking through for Sarah...."

"They got everything at the Library of Congress. All you got to do is find it. Come on, I'll take you inside."

They crossed the street, skirted a large fountain where a metal-green woman rode a seahorse, and mounted the granite steps to the main entrance. Edie stared at the gorgeous women carved into the big brass doors.

"This place is full of women," said Anabelle. "Wait 'til you see the ones inside."

She led Edie into a hallway with a mosaic floor and a high domed ceiling. Anabelle was right—the walls were lined with paintings of women.

"I call it the goddess temple," whispered Anabelle. "Come on, there's more to come."

She led her down a long hallway, right up to a door marked NO ADMITTANCE EXCEPT TO AUTHORIZED PERSONNEL. Edie hung back.

"Don't worry," said Anabelle. "We're authorized, we're U. S. citizens."

She pushed open the door, and they entered the main hall. Edie gasped. She'd only been in one library before in her life—the little two-room stone building in White River, open three afternoons a week from two to five and Saturday mornings from nine to twelve. She used to go there as a kid and wander through the six aisles, taking down from the shelves whatever book struck her fancy. When she needed something particular for a school project, the librarian would go with her and help her find it. This wasn't the White River library. She couldn't even see a librarian, and where were the books? All she saw were long tables with people sitting at them and great wooden cabinets where people were pulling out little drawers and flipping through the cards in them. It wasn't even quiet like libraries were supposed to be. A continuous buzz of voices echoed to the vaulted ceiling. Edie stood rooted to the floor, staring. Anabelle took her by the arm and pulled her along.

"Here's where the card catalogs by author begin," she said, waving at the first row of cabinets. "But if you don't know the author you're looking for, you go to the subject catalog, which should be in this direction."

Anabelle led her past row after row of the wooden cabinets. At the Ls, Edie stopped.

"I can't do it," she whispered. "I don't even know what I'm looking for."

"Well, we can ask one of the librarians over there."

Anabelle gestured to a high circular desk in the middle of the floor. Several women inside of it were looking at the scraps of paper people were handing them and giving them back other scraps of paper. Edie felt a band begin to tighten around her chest; the words she was about to speak stuck in her craw. She pulled away from Anabelle and half ran across the open area to the door, down the hallway lined by the painted ladies, across the mosaic floor of the entrance gallery, past the guard. Outside, she leaned against the fountain and gulped for air. Anabelle caught up with her.

"Hey, don't let it get to you. It's just a library like any other library only a little bit bigger. Course, even if you do know what you're looking for, it might take a week to get it. This is the main building, and there's an annex, and then there's another piece of it across the river in Virginia. It's all there, though, anything you could possibly want."

Anabelle's eyes were laughing. Edie dug her hands in

her pockets and stared down at a crack in the sidewalk.

"Don't worry about it." Anabelle's voice was gentler, and she touched Edie's arm. "You don't have to do it all right now, you know. There's time. I spent six years, and it wasn't all searching. Lots of time was spent just standing back and waiting and trying to figure out what to do next. Come on, I'm starving, let's go find somewhere to eat."

Anabelle directed Edie up Wisconsin Avenue to a small Japanese restaurant where she proceeded to order sushi and beer.

"What's that?" asked Edie, suspiciously, remembering the forkless food of the night before.

"Sushi is sushi and beer is beer, you'll find out when you eat it."

"Yeah, well, it'd better have something better than pie dough to eat it with."

"Hey, don't be a hick!" laughed Anabelle. "There's more to life than steak and potatoes. This is a cosmopolitan city with international cuisine, why not relax and enjoy?"

Edie felt her cheeks flush. "If you're embarrassed to be with me," she said angrily, "just say so, and I'll hit the road for home." She half rose in her seat.

"Whoa back a minute," said Anabelle, her eyebrows disappearing under the curls on her forehead. "Don't take my mouth so seriously, I call everybody names. How can you think I'm embarrassed to be with you? You're the most interesting person I've been with in years. Can't you tell? I like the country in you—you're genuine, like few people I know."

Edie slumped back in her seat. "I dunno, I feel like your friends at the house think I'm weird. I saw that one with the long braids rolling her eyes when I was fixing the faucet this morning, I've seen that look before."

"You worry about that? Those slickers never saw

anybody fix anything before, that's all. She probably thought it was politically incorrect to do anything that might benefit the landlord, even though it'll be a cold day in hell before he ever fixes anything. Anyway, they're not my friends, they're just some people I rent a room from when I'm in town. Who cares what they do with their eyes? Forget them."

Just then a kimonoed waitress arrived and set down a red-and-black lacquered tray filled with little party-type appetizers. It was colorful enough, although Edie noticed there still weren't any forks. It looked like Anabelle was bound to have her eating with her fingers. Edie picked one up and popped it into her mouth.

Anabelle watched her closely, her eyes twinkling. "How do you like the yellowtail?" she asked.

"It's okay," Edie answered, trying to imagine what the smooth taste rolling around her tongue was. "What is it?"

"Raw fish."

Edie choked. She couldn't decide whether to swallow or spit it out.

"Raw fish? You let me put raw fish in my mouth? I don't even feed my cat raw fish."

"How else was I going to get you to try it? Go on, admit you like it."

"No way. I ate meatballs with my fingers for you last night, but raw fish is too much. Next restaurant we go to is gonna be someplace with steak and baked potatoes, I don't care how hick it is. I've had enough foreign cooking to last me a lifetime."

Anabelle shrugged and began to eat the remaining sushi. Edie drank her beer and watched her lift the delicate pieces with a pair of chopsticks and place them carefully into her wide mouth. She almost wished she hadn't been so quick to dismiss the food, but not enough to swallow her pride and try again. She was still trying to figure out whether Anabelle was making fun of her or whether she ate in these kinds of places all the time. But Anabelle had just said she liked her, she found her interesting. As she watched Anabelle wrap her lips sensuously around each dainty piece of fish, she felt her heart beating queer little thumps and the blood creep slowly up her face. She ordered another beer and drank it down quickly.

When the sushi tray was empty, they left the restaurant and began walking, heading off the avenue onto the quieter neighborhood streets. They were admiring the flower displays and elegant houses when Anabelle turned to Edie and said,

"Tell me some more about your life in Vermont. You told me how you discovered jazz, but what about before that? What about your family?"

"Not much to tell," Edie responded. "Not much happened. We lived, we ate, we slept."

Anabelle pressed her. Edie finally started telling her about her early childhood in White River. As she talked, she realized she had something in common with Aunt Flo—the war years had been good years for them both. Aunt Flo had been working with all her girl friends, making money and having a good time without any men around. For Edie, those years had been an all-female society, too—just her mother, her sister and herself living in a small house on the bank of the White River.

"We were all pretty happy then," she told Anabelle. "When my father enlisted, my mother took over his job at the bakery on Main Street. She'd get us up with her at four in the morning and braid our hair and kiss us and put us back to sleep. An older girl in the neighborhood walked us to school, but at three o'clock in the afternoon she'd be waiting for us at the edge of the school yard. She'd ask us about our day all the way home. She'd sing to us while she cooked supper—usually boiled potatoes and cabbage, but she served it up like it there was roast beef with it. Then at bedtime she'd read us adventure stories—*Call of the Wild* and Jack London."

Edie had almost forgotten those days. She could see her mother, her face lively and laughing, her hand always ready to brush away tears. It had all changed when the war ended. Edie's father had come home. Edie hadn't remembered him too well, but Iola had told her how much fun he had been—he had tossed them in the air and carried them on his shoulders. But that wasn't the man who came home. Joe Cafferty had come home limping and silent and had spent most of his days sitting in a corner smoking cigarettes and coughing. Or he'd simply disappear, sometimes for a week at a time. Then her little brothers had come, one right after the other, four in four years. Her mother's smile had been replaced by a tight, worn look. She was often cross with the girls. She scolded them whenever they made any noise, saying the house had to be kept quiet for the sake of her father.

By the time Edie was ten, her father wasn't working any more. Nobody ever said why. She and her sister just supposed it was because he was sick so much, coughing and spitting phlegm. Her mother had gone back to the bakery, leaving the house at four A.M. again. Only now she never waited for them after school nor sang while cooking supper nor read stories before bed. Edie and Iola were expected to take care of the house, mind the babies, do the ironing, wash the dishes. The scoldings often turned into real anger. The two sisters learned to stay more than an arm's length from their mother at all times.

"If I really think about it," Edie told Anabelle, as they found a large flat stone to sit on in the Dumbarton Oaks

Park, "I can't really blame her. She had wanted to be a teacher. Her father had been a teacher, her mother had had a couple of years of college. But she came out of high school during the depression, so she ran off and got married instead. Her parents were furious. I guess by the time she had six kids and a sick husband she probably regretted it, but she never said anything. She didn't get any real support from anybody. Except for Aunt Flo, my father's family didn't like her because she never converted and didn't bother to send us to mass. *Her* family disapproved of her because they thought she married beneath her. My dad never did anything except smoke cigarettes and watch TV, my brothers were all hellions, and my sister and I did as little as we thought we could get away with, and then we'd take off running."

Edie scooped up a handful of stones and started tossing them, one by one, against an old black walnut.

"I suppose she'd had her dreams in us when we were little," she continued. "Maybe she still had them when we got older. I got pretty fair grades, and I remember a couple of times she looked at my report card and asked me if I wanted to go to college and become a teacher or something. I didn't think much of it, nobody I knew ever went to college, and there wasn't money for movies, let alone tuition."

Edie remembered the few times her mother had tried to talk to her about her future. She'd been puzzled and suspicious, waiting for an angry word and making excuses to get away. She frowned as one of the pebbles went wide of the tree.

"When I got pregnant, she really lost it. I didn't tell her until I started to show—hell, I didn't know it myself until I started to show. She questioned me, and I lied. She dragged me down to the doctor. The way she beat me, I couldn't tell whether she was angrier because I got pregnant or because I'd lied to her. Then when I ran away from the nuns and Aunt Flo wouldn't send me back, I guess she really went off the deep end. Iola had left home by then, she'd run off to San Francisco with the man she'd been going out with. So Ma was left alone with the four boys."

"Did you ever get to talk to her about it later?" asked Anabelle.

"She never forgave me. Tell you the truth, I didn't make it easy for her. After I lost the kid, I got into a bike crowd. And...I can hardly believe I did this, but when my dad died, I rode that Harley-Davidson up to White River. Missed the funeral and got to the house just in time for the wake. The whole Boston side of the family was there. My mother's in the kitchen muttering and complaining, and I walk in, all decked out in a black leather vest, no shirt and sunglasses, showing off this tattoo on my arm."

Edie pulled up her sleeve and flexed her bicep. A long black and red snake writhed over the words 'Don't tread on me.' Edie looked carefully at Anabelle.

"Did you ever do something in your life that was so stupid that it made you ashamed, really ashamed of yourself?" Edie stared at a flowering azalea. "Like, yeah, you were young and rebellious, but some things even rebellious kids oughta respect? Well, that's the one I'll never get over. My mother stopped her muttering and looked me straight in the eye with the coldest fury I've ever seen or hope to see. She didn't say a word, just left the house and disappeared for the entire wake. Somewhere in my dumb block head I could sense that having a baby and stealing from the poor box was bad, but what I'd just done was really unforgiveable. And it was. She never spoke to me again. She died a few years later, walked right in front of a train. My brothers got parceled out amongst the Boston aunts and uncles until they were old enough to be on their own. My sister stayed in San Francisco."

Edie was out of breath. She stopped and let her eyes drift over the bright azaleas nodding in the afternoon breeze. She realized she was tired, she couldn't lift her eyes from the pulsing colors. She felt Anabelle's hand close over hers, gently holding it. She lay back and closed her eyes. The birds overhead sounded far away, the children's shouts as if from another land. Anabelle's hand was soft and warm and comforting as she drifted away.

Edie dreams. But this is not a dream, this really happened. I am eight years old, and I am standing next to the piano in my grandmother's parlour. Iola is showing me something she's learned from a girlfriend at school. She tries the notes, falters, tries again, hits more wrong notes. She raises her hands once more and frowns in concentration. Her hands remain frozen over the keyboard as the sound of my grandmother's voice cuts through the air like a razor. "You've made your bed, Emily, now you can lie in it." "Mother!" My mother's voice is angry and humiliated. A second later she is marching through the parlour, gripping Iola's and my arms. We endure the pain as she drags us from the house. All the way down the hill to our house we half stumble through the snow. Her face is set in rage, and we already know enough not to struggle. Later that night, after a supper of cold potatoes and no father, we lie in the iron frame bed together and listen to her muffled weeping.

Edie opened her eyes. Anabelle was sitting a few feet away, watching her.

"You know," Anabelle said, "there probably wasn't anything you could have done to make your mother's life more bearable. When things get too awful for men, they can always just walk out. Either they disappear altogether—'G'bye, too bad things didn't work out so well,

91

think I'll try again somewhere else'—or they retreat behind a haze of smoke like your father did. Either way, they get to choose to not deal with life's problems. Once a man goes that route, there's not much a woman is going to do when she's got six kids. She just goes on putting one foot in front of the other, one meal on the table after the other. How can a child understand that?"

Edie looked up into the trees and watched a squirrel leap from one branch to another.

"Well, whatever, I can't change the way she was or the way I was." She paused. "I wouldn't mind seeing my sister again, though. We don't ever write, but Aunt Flo keeps me posted on what she's doing. She got married—not to the guy she ran off with but somebody later—and had three kids. She lives in Seattle now, works for Boeing. She's divorced, her kids are grown and gone. One of these days maybe I'll get my ass to the west coast."

"Maybe I'll get a gig out there, and we can go together," said Anabelle.

Edie looked at her and her heart jumped. Watch it, Edie, she said to herself, don't go getting excited at the thought of going to California together. The lady's celibate, she said so, and what's more, she's not even young and cute like you like them. Still…. Edie broke off her thoughts. Anabelle was pulling her to her feet.

"Come on, it's getting late. I gotta check in with the band. Let's get back to Sixteenth Street so I can get ready."

Edie was nervous as they entered the club. She'd never been around black people, she wasn't sure how they might take to her. Anabelle started to steer her to a table, but Edie hoisted herself onto a barstool and said,

"I think this feels more like home to me."

The club was fairly quiet. There were some people at a

couple of the tables, a few more sitting at the bar. Edie ordered her Jack Daniels and waited. When the band finally started to play, she caught her breath. Anabelle was right about playing better with this group. There was no comparison with the way she touched the keys here and the way Edie had first heard her. Edie listened to number after number, barely moving a muscle. The club gradually filled up. Halfway through the first set, every table was full with quite a few people standing at the side. Edie liked the crowd—people occasionally exchanged words, but mostly they sat like her, leaning forward, listening, nodding when they heard something they liked.

By the end of the second set, Edie's head was full of new sounds. Usually an early-to-bed, early-to-riser, she wasn't tired at all. She sat with Anabelle, the rest of the band and their wives and girlfriends for an hour or so more, watching the band wind down by drinking beer and joking with each other.

They finally left the club around three and headed back to Sixteenth Street. Edie's body glowed as she remembered the different sounds. Then, as they passed under a street lamp, her mother's face flashed across the windshield. The glow she felt now connected to the glow she'd felt as a child singing in the kitchen. An old hidden grief seeped up through the good feelings, a grief that her mother's happiness had ended, that her mother had never known this kind of easy good time, that her mother was not here right now to share this moment. She looked over at Anabelle who sat humming and staring out the window.

"You played real well, Anabelle," she said softly. "I'm real glad to be here with you."

"Yeah, well, don't run back to Boston just yet. We're just warming up, wait 'til you hear us really play."

It didn't seem to matter how late they got in, Edie was always awake by six as the truck traffic built up on Sixteenth Street. No one else was an early riser, so she had the first floor common rooms to herself for a couple of hours. One of the walls was covered with photographs taken by one of the women in the house—black-and-white studies of nude women contorting their bodies in bare cornfields. Other walls held posters and cartoons and flyers announcing art openings and poetry readings. Tacked to the kitchen door was a review of a dance performance torn out of a newspaper with the word 'Crap!' scrawled across it in purple magic marker.

Around eight, the house would start to come alive: toilets would flush, showers would run, the coffeemaker would start dripping. None of the women seemed to have a regular job—they were in and out at all hours, always in a hurry, calling out to each other that they were late for a meeting, they were expecting a phone call, they'd be back around seven. A large bulletin board next to the front door attempted to sort out all the activities, announcing who would be where when and whose job it was to mop the kitchen floor. Once a week they all sat down to dinner together and spent the rest of the evening hashing out the problems of the past week and anticipating the ones to come.

Edie found it overwhelming. Except for periods of close monogamy, she'd always lived alone. She'd never known people who came and went without stopping for a cup of coffee and a chat. She took to leaving the house just before eight to avoid the morning chaos and taking a walk in Rock Creek Park. As she walked, she often thought about Sarah. She'd tried to talk with Anabelle a couple of times about what kind of research she should be doing, what kinds of records they had here in Washington. Anabelle had said sure, there was all kinds of stuff, that Washington was nothing but a repository for records. But each time Edie had tried to pin her down, she'd veered off the subject and launched into other plans for the day. It seemed like, with her own search in a holding pattern, Anabelle didn't want Edie going off on her own. She guessed it didn't matter too much, there was no hurry really, and every day with Anabelle brought a new adventure.

One morning Edie came back to the sound of voices raised in argument.

"So what do you care what he says? He's a dummy jerk-off prick, everybody knows that. His wife once did a research project on Martha Graham, that qualifies him as a dance critic. Why do you pay any attention?"

"Because if I don't get good reviews, I don't get grants," a tight angry voice responded. "And if I don't get grants, I can't hire rehearsal space and dance. And if I can't dance, I don't get reviews of any kind." A short round woman with deep-set eyes was arguing with Anabelle.

"That's bullshit. When I first met you, you were dancing and you didn't get any reviews. Then you danced and got lousy reviews. Then you went to New York and a real critic saw you, so when you brought the show back home, El Jerko babbled on about how intriguing you were. The point is, you've been dancing all along. The reviews are irrelevant. You just want to create an intelligent being out of an asshole, and I got news for you, it ain't gonna happen."

"Well, goddamn it, I don't know why he can't see what's right in front of his eyes. Even when he thinks it's good, he misses the point. I'm sick of reading his crap."

"And I'm sick of hearing you say you're sick. Why don't you quit bellyaching about the Washington Post. You've been pissing and moaning for years now, he's not important, dancing is, so dance."

Anabelle looked up, saw Edie and threw up her hands in disgust. The dancer moved her angry body off to the kitchen.

"'Bout time you got back." Anabelle's voice was sharp and her eyes flashed anger. "I got posters to hang downtown, come on, we'll take the bus."

Edie could see that Anabelle was in one of her moods. Easy to get along with most of the time, Anabelle's face would suddenly glare and her mouth would let loose a stream of abuse. The moods seemed to come out of nowhere and vanish as quickly as they came. Just yesterday, when Edie said excuse me to a teenager who'd pushed in front of her at a drugstore counter, Anabelle had turned and snarled, "You backwoods booby, you wouldn't say boo to a goose, would you!" By the time the words had sunk in enough for Edie to react, Anabelle had pulled a *New Yorker* off a rack and was laughing at one of the cartoons. When Edie had demanded, "What did you mean by that?", Anabelle had only looked puzzled, then shrugged her shoulders and smiled a forget-it smile.

Today Anabelle's bristles were palpable. At the bus stop, the posters in her arms started to slip as a man brushed by.

"Watch out, you fucking asshole!" she yelled, trying to hold on to the posters. "What the sweet Jesus you think you're trying to do, elbow your way to hell?"

The man had stopped to apologize, but when he saw Anabelle's anger, he moved on quickly. Anabelle muttered invectives as she gathered her posters together. A bus finally pulled up, and people jostled for a place in the line. As Anabelle stepped up and threw in her change, one of the quarters missed the till and rolled across the aisle and under a seat. Anabelle dug into her pocket for another one and came up with only a dime. She threw it in and started to move on.

"Another fifteen cents, lady," said the young man at the wheel.

"I don't got another fifteen cents, fucker, it's under your goddamn seat. You wanna give me change, here's a five-dollar bill. Otherwise, shove it."

"Fifteen cents in the till, lady, or else step off. There's people waiting."

"You and the mayor and the whole city council can all go fuck yourselves to death. Exact change, you think we're all fucking money changers, we walk around with exact change in our pockets, every time we want to ride a bus we got exact change?"

Edie stepped up, firmly took Anabelle's arm and shoved two dollar bills into the till.

"Keep the change, mister. Come on, Anabelle."

She steered her to the back of the bus, and they sat down.

"Hey, what's up? The bus driver didn't make the rules."

"You can bloody go to hell with the rest of them. I'm sick of being pushed around by this fucking city. You want to criticize, you can take your hayseed hands and go jerk off the mayor with the rest of them."

Yesterday's sarcasm seemed like a gentle glancing blow compared to this direct onslaught. Two red spots appeared on Edie's cheeks, and she held her breath to prevent the tears that stung her eyes from overflowing. Her reaction puzzled her. It wasn't as if nobody had ever said a harsh word to Edie. As a kid, she'd learned to be deaf to her mother's harangues. When she'd fought with lovers, she'd always dished out as good as she got. Anabelle wasn't even a lover. Except that, when she'd touched Anabelle's arm to steer her down the aisle, she'd felt a warm rush, a pleasure in the touching. She sat staring at the floor, confused. Anabelle's voice, bright and cheerful, broke into her thoughts.

"Here's our stop. Let's go hang these posters. Then we can spend the rest of the day loafing."

They got off the bus, and Edie gave herself over to the task of tacking up posters in the several bookstores and restaurants they stopped in while Anabelle chatted with the management. After about six stores, Anabelle guided her to a street corner and said,

"All right now, I'm going to show you the gates of Hell. Here we are, I give you…the Dupont Circle Metro!"

It did indeed look like a descent into the lower depths. The escalator stretched downward forever while the great concrete bandshell entrance gave one the sense of entering a sterile cavern of the doomed. People pushed past them on the narrow escalators, too hurried to let the slowly moving stairs take them down. Edie thought she'd gotten used to the noise and crowding of the city, but this was more than she could handle. Dizzy, she held on to the rail with both hands. They finally reached the lower level.

"Where are we going?" she asked.

Anabelle didn't answer. She led them to a line at an information booth that inched up slowly. When their turn finally came, Edie couldn't understand a word of the directions.

"Did you understand her?"

Anabelle still didn't answer. As they pushed through the crowds, Edie began to sense Anabelle's anxiety.

"Tickets, we gotta get tickets," Anabelle was muttering as they found themselves in front of a bank of monster machines.

"How do they work?" asked Edie.

"I did this once before, look, there are children doing it, anyone can do it. Put your money in this slot, it says. You got a couple of ones?"

Edie handed over the dollar bills. Anabelle put one in. The machine rejected it. She put it in again. The tray came sliding out again. She tried the other bill. The machine treated it the same. Her muttering became angrier. She slammed the tray in and out. It stuck halfway with the dollar bill in it, the words OUT OF ORDER flashed on red. They could hear a train screeching its brakes. Anabelle kicked the machine and screamed at it and banged it with her fists.

"Motherfucker, give it back. You can't be out of order, I just gave you money, give me my ticket."

Edie pulled herself out of her own confusion and put her arm firmly around Anabelle's shoulder. She fought their way back through the crowd, not knowing where the damn escalators were but not allowing herself to panic. Anabelle had stopped struggling and was letting Edie pull her along. Finally Edie spotted a sign that said ELEVATOR and maneuvered them to it. Out of breath, she pushed the button. Magically the doors parted. As the doors closed behind them, she pulled Anabelle to her and put her arms around her.

"It's all right, Anabelle, we're almost out of this hellhole. We'll take a cab to wherever you want to go. Come on, Anabelle, it was just a damn machine, who needs it?"

Anabelle's shaking subsided as the elevator rose slowly to ground level. Out in the sunshine again, she smiled again and waved her hand as if to say, Not to worry, it was nothing.

"I dropped the posters anyway. Let's go sit in the park."

She led Edie to the fountain in the middle of Dupont Circle, and they sat down on the concrete edge. The sun warmed their backs, the subway experience receded into a half-remembered nightmare. Anabelle spoke.

"I can't deal with this subway. New York, Boston, they're dirty and they smell of piss, but they're human. Some little man or woman is sitting behind a cage pushing tokens at you. Maybe they talk a foreign language at you when you ask directions, and maybe they're surly and rude, but they're recognizable as human beings, they've got eyes and ears and arms and legs just like you and me. But great Father Washington, the city with one of the highest unemployment rates in the country, has to build a subway that uses machines instead of people. Machines that don't work half the time. Machines that flash 'out of order' at you just when your train is coming in...."

Anabelle's hands were waving and her voice was rising again. Edie reached over and grabbed one of them midair and brought it down firmly.

"That's enough," she said gently, but it was a clear imperative. Anabelle stopped talking and let her other hand drop to her lap. After a while she said,

"You're right. I yelled at the bus driver, too, and he was a human being."

Anabelle paused and studied the water in the fountain.

"I dreamed about my mother last night," she said finally. "She was on a stage dressed up in a Victorian gown made of brown satin with buttons all down the back. I was in the wings trying to see her face, but her back was to me. Every time she turned, one of the other actors would be standing between her and me, so I still couldn't see her. Then I realized the stage was empty, the actors had all gone home, and I was still standing in the wings trying to see her face."

Anabelle kicked off her shoes and swung her feet over the fountain edge and into the water.

"Pretty transparent, huh? I mean, I really want to know who this woman is. And the goddamn courts and social workers keep getting in my way. You know, when you were talking about your mother, those early years when you and your sister and your mother were having a good time together...I felt real jealous. My parents were good people, they took good care of me, but somehow...I never felt connected with them. I mean, I loved them and all, but there wasn't any strong feeling there. I wasn't unhappy, but I don't remember having a really good time until the summer Mattie came out. Now ever since I started this search, I've felt like there's this...almost connection, if I could find out just her name, somehow the links will come together. You've had your connection, now I want mine."

Edie was still holding Anabelle's hand. She ran her fingers down the length of each sinewy finger.

"You will, Anabelle," she said. "Be patient. You waited for years before you even started looking. It's only a week now, you'll know soon enough. You can do it with your eyes closed."

"Don't you want to know about your daughter? Aren't you impatient to find out who she is? Don't you feel some kind of connection to her?"

Edie frowned. Usually, Anabelle changed the subject whenever she mentioned her daughter. But now she seemed really interested.

"Well, I haven't hardly begun to look. I never even thought about her for thirty-odd years. And then one night, I was telling a story at Rosie's bar—Rosie's a friend of mine who runs a women's bar out of a fancy country inn run by a couple of gay guys—anyway, I was getting drunk one evening because some woman had just left me, and I found myself telling everyone about this kid I'd had. I guess she must have been in the back of my mind, or telling that story wouldn't have made such a difference. I didn't even know I was going to quit my job until I called my boss and told him off. But once I did that, I just kept going. Now, I don't know, I seem to have hit a dead end. When I called you, I guess I was hoping you could give me some ideas."

She paused and watched a paper cup floating in the water.

"Yes," she continued, "I do feel that connection you're talking about. I had her for almost four months, I can still remember locking eyes with her and the way her little hand would hang on to my finger for dear life."

They both sat with their feet in the water and their hands touching. The city continued pulsing its life around them, but they ignored it and let the afternoon slip away. They talked lazily—about the weather, about the women in the house, about the restaurants they'd been to. Edie couldn't remember anyone she'd enjoyed being with more. Even Anabelle's anger didn't seem so bad, she didn't seem to mean it personally, and it never lasted long. Edie felt she could sit here touching Anabelle's hand forever.

"Hey, let's head on uptown before the five o'clock rush starts." Anabelle broke into her thoughts. "We can hop a bus straight up Connecticut Avenue and hit a steak house that'll satisfy your craving for A-mur-ican food. Cross my heart, I promise not to yell at the driver and I won't call you a hick."

They put on their shoes, and Anabelle skipped across the circle, singing like an eight-year-old getting out of school. Edie ran to catch up.

It was early morning. Edie lay awake, listening to the trucks roar down Sixteenth Street, listening to Anabelle breathing softly beside her. They'd been in Washington almost two weeks now. Edie was thinking how utterly different these days were from anything in her life before. She was getting used to the strange rhythm of the house. All the women were intensely involved in the arts, although none of them seemed to have the kind of fun Anabelle had. In contrast to the frantic comings and goings of the rest of the house, Anabelle slept late, took Edie around to see the sights, dropped in on old friends, sat in Rock Creek Park watching the kids chuck stones into the water. After dinner she would go to the club, joke with the bartender, chat with the owner, talk with the other musicians as they wandered in. One by one they'd take to their instruments, and, at some unannounced time, they'd suddenly start playing. Only at that point did Anabelle get intense. She became an extension of her instrument, letting the sounds pour out. She seemed connected to each of the other musicians, too, taking riffs from one direction, transforming them, tossing them out in another direction.

Edie had never seen a jazz group play night after night.

The few times she'd gone to jazz clubs in Boston, she'd been so excited to see and hear the musicians in person, she hadn't actually thought about how the music was made. Watching this group, she realized that she'd learned a lot from Anabelle, and what she'd learned made what she heard even more interesting. The group seemed to really enjoy playing with each other. If one of them played a particularly nice passage, the others would nod in admiration. It didn't seem to matter to them much whether the audience liked what they did. They barely acknowledged the applause and played the same whether the audience was with them or being rowdy.

Edie was comfortable at the club. There were only a few white faces there, but mostly people were friendly. Some of the other customers responded with real warmth when she shared her enthusiasm for the music. Once, when she had been applauding vigorously for a rousing drum solo, the young man standing next to her had sneered, "What you know, white woman?" and moved away with his friends. But then the bartender had caught her eye and shrugged a 'those kids' shrug at her, and she had thought of some of the young toughs at Rosie's.

For the most part, sitting on a barstool sharing something with strangers who were friendly in an anonymous way didn't seem to be all that different whether the barstool was in a black club on Georgia Avenue or a lesbian bar in the mountains of Vermont. Up there strangers drank together and shared their enthusiasm for one ball bouncing other balls into some sidepockets. Here the same kind of people in different skins nodded to each other when an improvisation stretched a familiar tune into new territory. She felt at home. The bonus was that she got to watch Anabelle for four hours straight, watch her wonderful hands dance up and down the keyboard, watch her whole body animate the music.

Edie turned onto her side and looked at Anabelle now. She thought about how much she'd come to care for her. Sharing a bed with her every night without touching her was getting to be difficult. Yet she hesitated to make a move. She'd always kept her friends and lovers separate before. She'd had friends like Rosie that she'd been close to for years, but she'd never once thought of her as a potential lover. Women like Dawn, with whom she had little in common, were lovers only. If they were talkers, she'd listen, but she never talked about herself to them. Here was somebody she felt close to as a friend, and her body was responding as if she were a lover. She was grateful for Anabelle's declared celibacy, it set the boundaries in a familiar way.

As Edie lay musing, she heard Anabelle whimper in her sleep. Oh yeah, she thought, today's the big day. Adoption Agency Day. Anabelle's gonna go find out who she is. She's probably scared. Anabelle whimpered again, more insistently. Edie put her arm around her and pulled her close.

"It's okay, babes," she murmured. "Everything's gonna be all right."

Anabelle shuddered in her sleep, then opened her eyes slowly. Fear mingled with determination in them. Edie brushed her lips over Anabelle's forehead.

"Go back to sleep. It's early yet."

Anabelle nestled closer to Edie.

"Edie," she whispered.

"I'm here."

Anabelle lifted her head slowly and turned sleepily toward Edie. Her lips brushed Edie's and, startled, Edie pulled back. She heard Anabelle say,

"I want to make love to you, Edie."

Anabelle suddenly rolled over on top of Edie. Confusion exploded in Edie's mind. As Anabelle's tongue found its way into her mouth, Edie's body wanted to respond. But lying on her back with someone on top of her was eerie. Anabelle's large frame weighed her down, she felt like she was suffocating. No, it wasn't Anabelle's weight that was making her mind race, it was the lying back, the letting someone else take charge. Anabelle was nuzzling her nipple now, pulling it gently with her teeth, then kneading it with her lips. Edie liked the sensations, but she felt so helpless lying on her back. As Anabelle's strong hand began to caress Edie's inner thigh, Edie stiffened. It was too much, it was too difficult, she couldn't do it.

"What's wrong, woman?" murmured Anabelle. "Don't you want me? Don't you like the touch of my hand?"

"Yes...but...I...um...you're...I...."

Anabelle brought her lips close to Edie's.

"You feel so fine to me, Edie. I want you, I've wanted you all week. And I feel you wanting me. Don't tell me to stop."

Edie was embarassed. What could she say? Yes, she wanted to make love with Anabelle. But she wanted to do the lovemaking. No, that wasn't quite true, she liked what Anabelle was doing, she liked those long firm fingers moving over her body. How could she tell Anabelle that she'd never done this before? She closed her eyes and lay back.

"Don't stop," she whispered. But when Anabelle began to move her lips down Edie's belly, Edie's body stiffened again. The wonderful floating sensations were replaced by fear. Anabelle laid her cheek against Edie's navel and held her fingers motionless.

"Better tell me what's up, Edie. I know I'm not ravishing a virgin, and I know you feel something for me. I can't be that terrifying."

Edie relaxed a little. She took a deep breath.

"Anabelle. I don't know how to say this. But I've never done this before. I mean, letting someone make love to me. I...."

Anabelle rolled onto her back and whooped.

"Edie Cafferty! You mean to tell me you're one of those stonedykes, one of those heavy duty bulldaggers? My god, woman, that went out with Eisenhower!"

Edie raised herself on one elbow.

"Yeah, so what if I am? I'm a damn good lover, nobody's ever complained. I never billed myself as sophisticated, I am who I am, take it or leave it."

"Whoa back a minute. I didn't mean to insult you. You just surprised the hell out of me. You're such a gentle loving person, I know you're a beautiful lover. But you've got to let other people love you, too. Loving's got to go both ways, it won't last long if it's always one way. Come on, let me show you."

Anabelle began stroking Edie's body and whispering to her, compelling her to relax. Edie finally let herself go, let the sensations take over, let her body float out into a deep blue space. It was like riding a wave in the ocean. Rising and falling, the long slow swell carried her up and let her flow gently down. The feelings intensified, abated, then lifted her up again. The woman who was guiding her was Anabelle, her friend, Anabelle her lover. The line between friends and lovers had vanished.

Finally Anabelle said, "That's enough now. We can't do this all day. There's things to do and places to go. The everlovin' adoption agency, for one, is supposed to tell me who I am today. I was supposed to be there by ten."

"Let me go with you, " said Edie. "I want to be with you when you find out."

Anabelle looked away.

"No, Edie," she said slowly. "This is something I started alone, and I have to finish it alone. I've been working up to this for six years now. I've got to do the job myself."

"You're right," said Edie. "It's your search. Just don't forget to come back to me."

Anabelle got dressed and dashed out the door. She yelled over her shoulder,

"See you for dinner."

Edie floated all day. She ran down the street to Rock Creek Park. It was hot and muggy, so she just sat on a bank and watched the creek burble over the rocks. She wanted to tell someone, but there was no one to tell. The women in the house were intense but not passionate. They talked about their lovers matter-of-factly, even the one who had just started a relationship. She wanted to laugh with someone, and she'd never seen any of them even crack a smile. She wished Rosie were here, they could hoist a beer to celebrate. She wondered what Rosie would think when she found out Edie's new state of touchableness.

She spent the whole day enjoying the silly feelings. Late afternoon she wandered back to the townhouse and waited. She picked up a book and flipped through it, then a magazine. She began to get impatient. Time for Anabelle to get back so they could do a little celebrating before clubtime.

By nine Anabelle still hadn't shown up. Puzzled, Edie took the truck over to the club. She must have run into somebody, she thought, or gotten held up somehow and gone straight to the club.

The band was already playing when Edie walked in. As soon as she heard them, she could feel something different in the air. She cocked her ear and listened. It was the music. They were really playing tonight. No, not they.

It was Anabelle. There were sounds coming out of that piano that Edie had never heard before. That no one else had heard before, apparently, judging from the way the house was still, listening. The rest of the band was holding back, just backing her up and nodding their heads in admiration. She was incredible. It was the *A Train,* the first piece Edie had heard Anabelle play in Somerville. Anabelle's solo went on for ten, fifteen, twenty minutes holding everybody spellbound. She finally crashed to an abrupt stop. Sweat was pouring off her brow. It was early yet, but the place was full and the applause was wild. Edie was proud of Anabelle, proud that she even knew such a musician, let alone was loved by her. She waved to her to join her.

Anabelle's eyes, slightly glazed, looked right through Edie. Then she went and sat down with the other musicians. Edie could see she was unsteady but…what was going on? She must have seen her. The floating feeling that had begun to have an edge of fear now blossomed into full panic. *Something has happened.* Edie got up reluctantly. A voice told her to leave, but she moved steadily toward Anabelle's table.

"Anabelle," Edie stood by Anabelle's chair and spoke softly. Anabelle turned slowly and stared hard and cold.

"Anabelle?" she echoed. "Anabelle? Who Anabelle? Don't see no Anabelle here. Anybody here know anybody name of Anabelle? That a whitegirl name. Ain't no whitegirl here. This table for black."

Edie's heart stopped. What was going on? What was she talking about?

"My name Annie, girl. You hear? Annie, a good black name. Annie Jones. Born three fifteen in the A.M. on January thirty in nineteen hunnert and forty-one. My mama name Annie, too. She black and she beautiful and that make me black, too. Black and beautiful, whitegirl. Sittin' here with my black and beautiful friends, making black and beautiful music. Got no time for white now, girl."

Edie's mind began to take in what had happened. The search for Anabelle's mother was over. She could hear the pain and anger behind the piercing look and the mock black English. To have been so close to black music, to black people, all her life, and not to have known she was one of them. Yet Edie's own pain was there, too. She'd fallen in love with this woman.

"Tell you what else, whitegirl," Anabelle continued. "Ain't got no father. Just a beautiful black mother. And ug-ly white skin. Know what that make my father, whitegirl? Charley. Yeah, Charley. Charley rape my mama, give me this ug-ly white skin. Two years after he rape her, he come back to pick up he belonging. Charley white, Annie white, Charley go poof, she turn Anabelle. Anabelle Whitegirl."

Edie felt paralyzed. She knew she had to get out of there, but she stood rooted, staring at Anabelle. No, it was Annie now. Anabelle who had said, I love you, this morning had turned into Annie who was saying, Go away.

"Well, now, poof, I turn Annie again," she heard over the roar in her ears. "No more white world. You go on back a your white world, this world no place for you. You killin' my people, you trying to kill me. But we ain't dyin' for ya. We livin', we strong. We got a strong music. You try a steal black music, we takin' it back. This music ain't for you. You Charley, rapin', killin' the whole world, we sayin' no, we gonna kill you...."

Tears were rolling down Anabelle's face now, and she started to choke. The tall bass player, who had been looking concerned since she started talking, stood up and pulled her to her feet.

"Come on, Annie, we got a set to play. Let's go get us some coffee."

Edie made herself turn and leave the club. Her face was a rock, her whole body was a rock. She felt nothing. No rage, no pain. She climbed into her truck and somehow managed to get it onto the interstate going north. Coming out of the Baltimore Tunnel, the tears started. Edie howled. By the time she got to the Delaware Bridge, she was hoarse. She jammed a Billie Holiday into the tapedeck and let the tears run down. She got to Boston just in time for the morning rush hour and didn't get to Aunt Flo's until almost ten. Exhausted, she threw herself down on the couch, kicked off her shoes and fell asleep.

Edie dreams. I'm in a foreign city with wide plazas and no trees. A cold wind makes me shiver. I climb onto a skateboard running over a track of marbles, and it takes me out of the city into a meadow with bright red flowers on tall stems. The smell is intoxicating, I feel dizzy. The skateboard circles back into the city which is now being destroyed. Great hulks of machinery lie upended. Divebombers drop explosives all around me. The skateboard track is destroyed, the marbles are scattered all over. As I pick my way through the wreckage, someone takes my arm and guides me to a woman I have seen somewhere before, but I can't remember who she is. 'This is the alto, she's the leader.' We climb on a skateboard together and push it over the rubble. I try to hold on to the woman, but the skateboard is broken in two, and her part is moving away rapidly. Bumping and bouncing, I call to her to wait for me.

Edie wasn't bouncing on half a skateboard, she was being shaken awake by Aunt Flo. She opened her eyes and slowly let Aunt Flo's wrinkled face come into focus.

"You were having a nightmare, Edie. I thought you'd best wake up."

"God, what time is it? How long have I been sleeping?"

"Well, I don't know what time you started, but it's ten o'clock now. You've been out to the world since I came home at six. I was going to wake you, but you looked like a mac truck wouldn't wake you. Here, drink this warmed-over coffee, get the grog out of your head."

Edie sat up and drank the stuff. That was one thing you could always count on, Aunt Flo's coffee. It was the same fresh or boiled over—strong and bitter and black.

"You should have left me a phone number where I could reach you. I've been waiting for you to call or write." Aunt Flo's voice was breathless. "I felt so bad after you left. It seemed like I was kind of responsible, and then I wasn't much help at all. It kept on my mind night and day. I thought if I could just help you with the search, it would help to make up for what I did before."

Edie stared at Aunt Flo. It seemed like she ought to

113

know what Aunt Flo was talking about, but for the life of her she couldn't put it together. Why did Aunt Flo think she was responsible for Anabelle? They didn't even know each other, Aunt Flo didn't know anything about Anabelle's search. Then Edie remembered Sarah. Her daughter. That was how all this had started. She was looking for Sarah. Anabelle came later. Sarah was the reason Edie left Vermont. Edie's current pain slid out of focus as she struggled to grasp what Aunt Flo was saying.

"You remember my friend Marge? With the granddaughter who's a lawyer? Well, we went out to lunch with her last week, and I told her about how that awful lawyer had treated you, and how you'd already checked out the church, so you didn't know what to do next. And she said, Marge's granddaughter—her name's Susan—she said that sometimes adopted children have special problems and turn up in juvenile court—that's where she works, in juvenile court."

Aunt Flo stopped.

"I'm sorry, pet, I'm going too fast. I just got excited when I thought about what she told me. She said we couldn't look through the juvenile records, but that she did know a social worker who's been in the system for years, somebody who has a remarkable memory for children she's worked with. She thought if you talked to her, you might find something. Here, I wrote down her name, it's Virginia Welles."

Aunt Flo handed Edie a slip of paper with a name and telephone number. Edie looked at her and then at the piece of paper. She didn't think she liked social workers much, it was a social worker who had carried Sarah out of her basement room and out of her life. But if this woman had ever run across Sarah, had any information about her, it would be nice to know it. It would get her mind off Anabelle, too.

"Thanks, Aunt Flo. I'll call her tomorrow."

Edie spent the night tossing. Images of Anabelle's face kept pushing away the thoughts about beginning the search again for Sarah. She saw Anabelle laughing, Anabelle frowning, Anabelle concentrating on her music, Anabelle telling her, I love you. The sequence always ended with Anabelle's face contorted in rage, the angry words spewing out of her mouth. Edie would roll over and bury her face in her pillow trying to block it out. She tried to rehearse the coming telephone conversation with the social worker, but it kept getting interrupted by Anabelle laughing, Anabelle frowning, Anabelle.... Daylight creeping through the windows was a welcome relief.

Edie waited until ten to call Virginia Welles. The woman had apparently been expecting her call. By ten fifteen Edie and Aunt Flo were on their way to the Charlestown City Hall.

"Come in, come in. I'm Virginia Welles. This is the little cubby hole they've put me in for the last thirty years. Just me and my desk and a hundred thousand manila folders. Sit down."

They sat down on the two folding chairs in front of the desk. The room was tiny, barely enough space for the desk and six file cabinets. The floors were the same linoleum as the hallway, a single window high on the wall gave a glimpse of ground level bushes. Virginia Welles wore a nondescript blue pants suit that hung loosely over her large frame. She peered over half glasses and stubbed a cigarette in the overflowing ashtray.

"Susan tells me you're looking for a daughter you gave up for adoption—in 1955, right?"

Edie nodded.

"Well, 1955, I hadn't graduated to this office yet, I was still in the main room with thirty other social workers. But Susan's idea was that your daughter might have had some problems with the authorities, and we might find her having passed through these hallowed halls. Problem number one, we don't know her adopted name. A fairly sizeable problem. How to find somebody whose name you don't know. Susan said your aunt gave your daughter's birthdate as sometime in January of 1955. That gives us an age at least."

Edie had never thought about Sarah's name. She was Sarah Cafferty, wasn't she? But of course, nobody knew that but her. Even Aunt Flo hadn't known then that she'd named the child Sarah. As for Cafferty, of course, adopted children take on the name of their adoptive parents. Her heart sank. This is impossible, there's no way to track her down, even if she did get into trouble with the law.

"Nothing's impossible, you know," Virginia Welles was saying, as if reading Edie's thoughts. "I was curious after Susan told me the story. So I ran a check. They got a computer system in here six years ago, and somebody keyed in all the cases from 1960 on. Name, birthdate, case number. I thought it was a waste of time, but I think it paid off in your case."

Edie looked at her. The woman's eyes were smiling at her over her glasses.

"There's a Mary Catherine Cafferty, birthdate given as January eighth, 1955. She appears in the records five times. I don't know if that's your daughter, and if it is, you'd better prepare yourself for a not too pleasant picture. Are you ready?"

Edie looked at Aunt Flo. She'd already accepted that her daughter might have been a juvenile delinquent. Now what?

"This Mary Catherine Cafferty first got into trouble in 1964. Running away from her foster home."

"Why was she in a foster home? Wasn't she adopted?"

116

asked Aunt Flo.

"I'm afraid that's the worst news. The computer listing gives only name, birthdate, birthplace and of course the court case number and date. The birthplace is usually listed as the city and state where the child was born. But in Mary Catherine's case, the birthplace is given as 'Saint E.' Now Saint Elizabeths was an orphanage that was closed in 1959. So my guess is that she was never adopted, she was first in Saint E's and from then probably in foster care. All of her cases are for running away. I'm sorry. Shall I go on?"

All these years, whenever Edie'd thought about Sarah, she'd assumed she'd had a better life than what she could have given her. That was the whole point, wasn't it? Angry and hurt as she'd been by Aunt Flo's actions, she'd always thought in some part of her that Aunt Flo had been right, that she couldn't properly care for the child, that the child was better off in a real family, in a house maybe, with enough money to buy good food and clothes. An orphanage! That was what that lawyer bastard had stolen her for? An orphanage? She took a deep breath and said flatly,

"Yes, I'm sure that's her. Give me the details."

"I really am sorry," said Virginia Welles. "There aren't any details here. Those would be in the actual case records which are filed away in the vault. Now you can only get into the vault with a court order—which I can tell you from experience is not easy to come by. But let me tell you what is clear from the computer records, and we can piece together a sketch of at least a few years of her life right now. Mary Catherine Cafferty was placed in juvenile detention five times, each time for running away from her foster home, each time a different foster home. She was eleven when she first ran away, the last occurrence that shows up is when she's fifteen."

Virginia Welles leaned back in her chair and lit another cigarette. She inhaled deeply and then went on.

"I can tell you from my own experience that children often run away from foster homes, not because the foster parents are terrible or mistreat them or anything, but because they've never had a chance to feel like they were part of the family. Sometimes it's the best foster parents they run from, because by the time they've been shifted from here to there a dozen times, they get to believing they don't deserve anything good. So when they get to a home that feels like a real home, they can't handle it, and they run away. I won't gloss over it, we've had some foster homes that were abusive, but by and large foster parents do the best they can. It's really us, the social workers, who are at fault for a lot of the trouble. We had policies for years that required kids being moved every year. The idea was that they not get too attached to any one home. So they got shuttled from one place to another every ten months or so."

Edie hunched her shoulders and stared at her shoes. Aunt Flo reached over and put her hand on her knee.

"Forgive me, pet. I was just a dumb scared woman. We could have brought that child up together. I just never thought anything like that could be done. I'm so sorry for you, for Sarah."

"None of us thought things like that could be done—until the sixties when people started doing it," said Virginia Welles. "But there's no use crying over spilt milk. The question is, where do you want to go from here?"

"Where can I go from here?" asked Edie, feeling hopeless. "How can I possibly find her? If the last time she got caught was when she was fifteen, then she probably finally made it when she was sixteen."

"You're right. There were thousands and thousands of runaways in the late sixties. Now you could go after a court order to get into those records and find out the names of her various foster parents. That might or might not help you find her. You might only get more background on her childhood. But you never know, she might've hit it off at her last foster home, and they might be still in touch. I can give you the name of a lawyer, if you want to try. But you may just want to start looking on your own. You have her name now. That's a start. Only a start, since she could have gone anywhere, New York, San Francisco and she could have changed her name many times."

Edie remembered the stories she'd heard at the Women's Center. Her stomach was starting to tie itself into knots. The room was overheated, and she could feel sweat running down her ribcage. Virginia Welles' words seemed to be coming from far away.

"If you want to make a search, prepare yourself for a long one. It can take years. But if you persevere, eventually you may get lucky. It's probably not something you'll want to do full time, but whenever you're in a city, start with the phone book. Check the voter registration lists. The Department of Motor Vehicles. Join an adoption society, go to their meetings, read their newsletters. Place an ad in their newsletters. Here's an old copy of one. Once you've contacted one group, they'll lead you to another."

Edie took the newsletter, folded it, stuffed it in her hip pocket, and stood up. She was angry. She didn't want to dump on this woman who had been helpful and sympathetic. But she had to get out of this suffocating room. She turned on her heel and left. Aunt Flo got up and started to thank Virginia Welles, but the woman waved her on.

"Go take care of your niece. She needs you."

Neither of them said much on the way back to the

apartment. Aunt Flo reached over and squeezed Edie's hand a couple of times, murmuring, I'm sorry. As the afternoon wore on, Edie's mood got uglier and uglier. She didn't want to take it out on Aunt Flo, she knew she was feeling as bad as she was. Getting drunk seemed like a good idea. Edie left the apartment and headed the pickup into town. As she drove, she could feel the stonedyke in her taking over. She gave the finger to three trucks in a row while muttering, Come on, Edie, babes, get your tough on. You don't need Anabelle, you don't need Sarah, you don't need anyone. You've got yourself, that's all you've got, and that's goddamn good enough.

Edie picked the sleaziest of the gay bars, one with men in make-up and high heels and any number of old familiar butch types. Edie didn't want any goddamn social work sympathy, she wanted a few rounds of good bourbon and a well played pool game. She figured she'd already gotten into the one-night stand stage of her life, so she armoured herself with swagger and started picking up women. Being in control again felt goddamn good. Edie picked her women out, paid for their drinks, invited them to the mattress in the back of her truck. Their screams of pleasure made her feel powerful and telling them when to go did, too. She still had almost five thousand dollars in her pocket. The way she felt, she could just stay here 'til she blew it all and then go back to bookkeeping in Owensville.

Edie stayed in the bar three nights running, leaving only when the bartender insisted, falling fully clothed onto her mattress and heading straight back in as soon as she woke up. Late in the evening of the third night at the bar, Edie was about to put the make on a beautiful little baby doll with spiky heels and pouty lips when a familiar voice sounded at her elbow.

"I shoulda known you'd pick a dump like this. Hey, bartender, two coffees and the check down this way."

Rosie perched her heavy frame on the barstool next to Edie. She let her steel-rimmed glasses slide down her aquiline nose and peered over them at Edie. She waved her hand in Edie's face.

"Hi there, I'm Rosie, remember me? I used to know you when."

Edie reached over to push her off the stool, lost her balance and grabbed the edge of the bar instead.

"Goddammit, Rosie, you spoiled my timing. Now she's letting that lady wrestler buy her a drink."

"Good luck for her, then, because you're on your way out anyway. Here, drink this and scour out your brain. What's she owe, bartender?" Rosie pulled out her wallet and started counting out dollar bills.

"Hey, wait just a goddamn minute, nobody buys my drinks for me, I pay my own goddamn way."

"Oh, shove it, Edie. Time you focus your eyes long enough to count your change, we could be halfway to Charlestown."

Edie dropped the act. This was Rosie, after all, there wasn't any need to prove anything to her. She downed the coffee and followed her out to the truck. When Rosie held out her hand for the keys, Edie dropped them in without saying a word.

"So how'd you find me?" Edie asked a little sheepishly as they pulled out into traffic.

"I had some business to do in Boston, I thought I'd just drop in for a visit. Your Aunt Flo said you'd taken off in a foul mood, so I figured it was binge-time for you. Then I got lucky, my cabbie was a dyke. I told her to skip the yuppie spots and concentrate on the dives. Gotcha second try. Now, you sober yet, you want to tell me what happened?"

Edie hunched into her seat. "Nothing happened," she mumbled. "She's gone."

"Yeah, your Aunt Flo told me. Tough break. But then, did you really expect to find her in three weeks? You've hardly started, don't tell me you're giving up already."

Edie didn't answer. Rosie drove for a while in silence. She turned onto Memorial Drive, found a place to pull the truck over and shut off the engine.

"Come on, Edie," she said. "This is Rosie. I've known you for twenty-odd years. And I've never seen you go on a binge except for one reason. Who was she?"

Edie still didn't say anything.

"Okay, I'm Nosy Rosie, so I'll just pry a little. Your Aunt Flo said you were in Washington for two weeks with a friend. She didn't tell me who the friend was because she didn't know, but she did say you came back looking like death warmed over. Then you got some bad news about your daughter, then you disappeared. Now I know you feel bad about your kid not getting a decent home. But that's not binge territory. I say the binge isn't over one Sarahchild unseen for thirty-two years. I say it's about some sweet body you went to Washington with and came back without."

Edie stared out at the Charles.

"Well," Rosie continued, "let's see. Every woman I've seen you with in the past three years has been a few years younger than the last. Since the last one I saw you with looked about eighteen, this one must have been underage. I say you're wanted in seventeen states for impairing the morals of a minor. The Supreme Court won't go easy on you, you know."

"Goddamn you, Rosie...."

122

"Hot damn, it talks! Come on, tell Rosie all the sweet and pungent details."

Edie started to clam up again. Then she threw back her head and laughed.

"Jesus, Rosie, you always did know how to put a needle in." Edie paused. "What the hell, it's no big deal. She's not the first woman who ever dumped me, and I don't suppose she'll be the last. But she was different." Edie watched a small boat with running lights make its way up the Charles.

"It wasn't the sex, Rosie. That wasn't even the biggest part of it. She was...she wasn't like anyone I've ever been lovers with. She was...she wasn't just someone you hop in the sack with, she wasn't...."

"Okay, Edie. I'm beginning to understand what she wasn't. Now why don't you start at the beginning and tell me all in a straight line: how you met her, what she said, what you said, what happened next. I'm too old for jigsaw puzzles."

"All right. She plays jazz piano. I met her when she was playing in a bar in Somerville. You know how I like jazz. I heard her though an open door and went in. We got to talking during the break, and it turned out she was a-dopted, she was on her way to Washington to get some information out of the agency that handled it. I'd already done a little asking around about Sarah, and I didn't seem to be getting anywhere, so I decided to go with her." Edie looked over at Rosie. "Just friends so far, Rosie. She wasn't my type at all. It was more like being with you— she was easy to talk to, we laughed a lot together, no bullshit feminism, either."

"What you got against feminism, Edie? Some of my best friends are feminists. Anybody asks me, I tell 'em I'm a feminist myself. You, too, even if you don't admit it."

"Yeah, well, maybe. But some of them make me uncomfortable with all their talk. I always feel like they're looking down their educated noses at me. Anyway, you wanted to know about Anabelle."

"That's her name?"

"Yeah, Anabelle." The sound of it was sweet. Then she remembered.

"Well, no, it's not. It's Annie." She stopped for a moment. "That's what she found out from the adoption agency, I guess. That she wasn't Anabelle, she was Annie."

Edie choked, turned it into a cough and blew her nose. Rosie let the silence sit for a while.

"Okay, you meet her, you're friends, she's Anabelle, then she finds out she's originally Annie. That's not so unusual, adopting parents changing a name like that."

"It wasn't just her name, Rosie. She found out...that her mother was black, that she'd been born black." Edie felt the tears welling, but she went on. "Her parents—she thought all along that they were so supportive, gave her all kinds of information about how she was adopted. Until she told them she wanted to see her original birth certificate. Then they clammed up, wouldn't even tell her the name of the agency they got her from. The thing was, they always made sure she had black friends, that they had black friends. They bought her a piano, gave her lessons, but when she got into playing jazz with black musicians, they wouldn't even come to hear her play once."

"And all along they knew she was born black?"

"Well, supposedly adoption agencies give you that kind of information, don't they?"

"Not necessarily. I had a cousin who adopted a kid, the adoption agency wouldn't tell her shit about the birth mother, told her the kid'ud be better off not knowing anything about her since the woman lacked the—quote, unquote—natural instincts of a woman. But what happened with Anabelle? When she found out?"

The tears behind Edie's eyes started rolling silently down her cheeks. She saw Anabelle/Annie reflected in the windshield, her broadly chiseled features twisted in rage. Or was it pain?

"We'd just become lovers, Rosie. We'd been friends before. We'd been sleeping in the same bed, but that was because the house we were staying in had only one spare bed. But I never touched her. I won't say it didn't cross my mind. It was a little confusing. Like I said, she wasn't my type at all, but I was really turned on. But she'd told me she was celibate and...hell, Rosie, she was a friend, like you. I've never made lovers out of friends—it doesn't work, you know that. When it's over, you lose the lover and the friend, too.

"Anyway, the morning she was due to hit the agency...look, Rosie, she started it and...it was so different from anything I'd ever felt before...." Edie remembered Anabelle's touch. Then she heard the angry, bitter words that drove her away. The two of them sat in silence watching a mist settle over the Charles.

"You haven't told me why you left or she left or whatever happened. You made love, and then she went off to chat with the adoption agency. And then...?"

"She didn't come back like she promised. We were gonna celebrate. So finally I went to her club where she was playing. And when I came in she was playing something incredible. You could feel it, everybody could. Then she stopped and...she turned on me, Rosie. She called me white and told me she didn't have room in her world for white. She told me to get out, to leave her to her people...."

Edie stopped. Rosie reached over, took her hand between her own two leathery ones.

"That was one helluva row to hoe, Edie," she said softly. She let the minutes pass. A soft rain had begun to fall. Together they watched the raindrops trickle down the windshield like tears. Then Rosie turned the key in the ignition, and the truck jumped to life.

"Well, you've had your binge, it's time to shoulder your ass. You can't leave her like that, you know."

"What do you mean, she doesn't want me."

"Shit, Edie, I ain't no psychologist, but that woman sounds like maybe if she doesn't want you right now, she sure as hell needs you. She must of been in some kind of shock. Let's see, how would that little frizzy-head from Ithaca put it? 'She was rejecting you because she was rejecting herself or at least the white part of herself. But she will have to integrate those two aspects of her self in order to achieve a wholeness....' Oh, hell, I can't keep it up, but there's always a little truth to that psychology crap. Look, you said she was celibate. Take it from me, celibacy means you don't want to get too close to anyone, friends are enough. So she hasn't planned on intimacy, but she falls in love with you anyway. Then she gets the shock of her life— 'Oops, we forgot to tell you, dear, you're black.' Would you expect her to act rational-like? Come on, Edie, use your noodle. Time to stop wallowing and start acting. I'd go with you except the weekend's coming up, and I got to get back to tend bar. Anyway, you probably need to do this one on your own. Let's go catch a few winks at your Aunt Flo's, toss around a few ideas tomorrow and then send you on your way. Since you don't know where to start looking for your daughter, you may as well start in Washington. Social Security, Census Bureau, I don't know. And while you're at it, you can look for your lover."

As Edie drove into Washington, hot sticky air flowed in through the truck windows and pressed around her. In the week she'd been gone, Washington summer had arrived. The leaves hung limply on the trees, exhaust from the cars turned the air blue. Edie took short shallow breaths, trying to breathe without choking on the fumes.

She and Rosie had decided that she should start at the house on Sixteenth Street. The women there were all white, so it wasn't likely that Anabelle had returned. Still, they might have heard something, or she might have come back to pick up her things. Edie knocked on the door nervously.

The short round dancer answered and looked at her coolly. "You're back for your stuff. Good thing, we've got a new housemate coming in."

"Has Anabelle been here?" Edie knew the answer, but she had to ask.

The woman raised an eyebrow slightly. "No, we thought she was with you. Oh, well, you'd better take her things with you when you go, we don't have any place to store them here."

Edie was glad to slip up the stairs to the little room on the third floor. She had thought she might stay there for a few days, but she could see she wasn't welcome. She'd have to figure out something else.

The room she'd shared with Anabelle was untouched from their morning of lovemaking. She saw it all as if she were looking through the wrong end of a telescope. Methodically, she packed their things into the two suitcases, straightened the room and left.

Next stop would be the club, but things wouldn't get going there until later. Edie wandered down Columbia Road looking for a place to eat. The street that had seemed so alive and colorful when she first saw it three weeks ago now seemed noisy and jarring. She ducked into a bar that had only a few people drinking late afternoon beers, relieved to be someplace dark and quiet. Even though the faces were mostly Hispanic, it felt familiar. By the time she'd finished her plate of red beans and rice and a couple of beers, she knew it was time to go.

She was scared but determined. Anabelle might still be playing at the club. If she saw her, there might be a repeat of last week's scene. On the other hand, what Rosie had said made sense, Anabelle had been acting pretty crazy. Who knows how the other musicians were taking it.

As she climbed the stairs to the club, she knew Anabelle wasn't there. The music floating down to her sounded pretty good, but the piano was drab with none of Anabelle's magic touch. Except for the piano player, though, the group was the same. Edie stood at the bar until the break and then approached the tall bass player, the one who'd acted concerned about Anabelle that night. He waved to her and pulled out a chair for her to sit down on.

"Looking for your friend?" he said after ordering two beers. "I'm sure glad. She needs somebody."

Edie said quickly, "Where is she? Where can I find her?"

"Can't tell you that, I'm afraid." He leaned back in his

chair. "Let's see, that little explosion happened last Friday night? So she stayed at my house that night. The wife wasn't too happy about it—her mother's in the hospital, the kids are just finishing school, her boss is breathing down her neck about a deadline. But we took her in. She was in real bad shape by the end of the evening. She couldn't play the second set—just vamped chords and kept wandering off into strange keys. Everybody was having a hard time following her."

The waitress set down two glasses and poured beer into them. The bass player drank deeply and then continued.

"So she came home with me. Next day she seemed okay, real quiet-like, played with the kids, did some shopping for us. Then bam! I don't know what somebody said, but she went off on a harangue about not trusting Charley and all that stuff she laid on you. And what us black folk should be doing about it."

The bass player smiled a tight smile.

"Hell, me and my wife both spent the sixties marching and sitting in, we don't need anybody telling us what to do about Charley. And that trip about her being black didn't go down too well either. Maybe her mama was black, but she's been passing all her life. She grew up white, she look white, as far as most of us are concerned, she is white. Don't matter to me nohow. I like her piano, black or white. She can make music, I don't care what color's her skin. But I don't need her giving me no Black Power trip."

Edie's heart sank.

"What happened?" she asked, afraid to hear the answer.

"Well, we really got into it. My wife and I were both born without a pot to piss in. We worked our butts off trying to make a decent home for our kids. It's an integrated neighborhood—there's not too many of them in

Washington—and we like it. Neither of us got to where we are by taking shit from anyone. I know your friend was in some kind of state, but when she started calling us oreos and saying she was gonna go find her some real black, we let her go. Of course, she didn't show up at the club that night, so we got Petey there to sit in. I don't know where she is, but I sure do hope you find her. She plays one helluva piano, and I don't like to see her go off the deep end."

None of what the bass player said surprised Edie, but it was hard to hear.

"Where do you think she might go? Where can I look for her?"

"I don't really know. If she's looking for all black, I guess there are a couple of clubs in Anacostia you might try. But you can't go there alone. You got any black friends?"

"I don't know anybody in this town," said Edie evenly. "You give me the names of the clubs, I'll find somebody black to go with me. Does it have to be a man, or can women go there?"

"I don't know as how Anacostia's safe for anybody, including the people who live there. Especially the people who live there. I'd say take a man, but you look pretty tough. Find you a black woman as tough-looking as you, maybe you'll be all right."

The bass player wrote down the names of two clubs with Southeast addresses. Then he added his own name and telephone number.

"We're only gonna be here through this week. If you need any help, give me a call. I may be going on the road, but my wife'll be here. She was pretty pissed at Annie, but she felt real bad, too. Good luck."

Edie shook hands with him and left the club. She was

worried about Anabelle, but she was also relieved to have found somebody else who cared what happened to Anabelle.

It was eleven o'clock. Edie was tired, but she didn't feel like checking into a hotel yet. Maybe she could find that women's bar she'd heard about. She got out a map of the city and finally located Half Street. Being Friday night, the club was jammed, and the music was ear-splitting. Edie pushed her way through sweating bodies until she got to the bar. She ordered her Jack Daniels and turned to watch the crowd. Next to her, someone was trying to tell a story to the busy bartender.

"...so I said, what if I sprung off the ladder like it was a diving board. 'Cause I'm not that high off the ground. So I go up and down like a diver and *boing!* I'm flying through the air straight up. The paint can's going down past me, so I grab it by the handle as it goes by, and I come down on the car, put the paint can down on the hood, roll off the car and onto the ground."

"I'd know that story anywhere," cried Edie. "What the hell are you doing here, Korba?"

The short wiry carpenter turned and slapped Edie on the back.

"Hey, Edie Cafferty! That story got me a beer in Vermont, what do you think it'll get me here?"

"Two beers at least. Set her up, bartender."

Edie and Korba moved off to the back of the bar where there were a couple of decibels less of music.

"So what are you doing here?" asked Edie.

"I got a construction contract here. I'm the one who should be asking you. You were on your way to Boston, last time I heard."

"I'm looking for a woman."

"Hey, aren't we all. Go ahead and look, it's free. It's doing anything else that'll cost you."

"No, seriously, I'm looking for a particular woman. Her name's Anabelle or sometimes Annie. She plays piano, and she's in trouble, I think. I don't know where to find her."

"What kind of trouble—legal?" asked Korba.

"No, not that kind. Emotional, I guess." Edie didn't want to go into the story again. She knew Korba would be sympathetic, but she didn't want to relive her own feelings. "She's had a kind of breakdown, I guess. Anyway, she's disappeared. Nobody knows where she is. I want to find her, and I've got a couple of leads, but I need somebody to go with me."

"At your service. This place is getting too smelly anyway."

"Yeah, thanks, but...," Edie stumbled a bit. "I need somebody black to go with me, I have to go to Anacostia."

"Oh, is your friend black?"

Edie frowned. She realized that she'd have to tell her. As she launched into the story, she was surprised, it was okay now. With her focus on finding Anabelle, her own feelings were under control.

Korba listened intently as Edie talked, asked a few questions and nodded her curly black head at the answers. When Edie finished, she looked at her watch and said, "It's midnight. I've got a couple of friends who might help, but they're working tonight. You got a place to stay?"

Edie shook her head.

"I'm staying up in Takoma Park—you'll have to sleep on the floor, but I think they'll put you up. I'll call my friends tomorrow morning, and tomorrow night we'll go bar hopping. Anacostia's not so bad, you just have to be careful. But that's true of most of Washington—or any damn city, for that matter."

T.J. and Delta were the names of Korba's two friends. T.J., built like a tank, had a sweet round face with a perpetual smile. Delta was older, tiny and had tough written all over her narrow face. They both wore black turtlenecks and denim jackets. They shook hands with Edie without saying anything, then squinted at the club names written on the paper Edie had handed them.

"Bubbles Lounge on South Street. I know where that is," said Delta. "We'll have to ask there about the other one." She eyed Edie's truck. "Looks like I'm on your lap again, Teej."

The four women climbed into the cab of the truck, and Edie followed Delta's directions. They crossed the bridge into Anacostia, and Edie maneuvered the truck through streets littered with garbage, lined by street lamps that mostly didn't work. She pulled up in front of a pink stucco building with a green neon outline of a naked woman. One of the windows had a Pabst sign in it, the other was boarded over. The four women trouped in together and headed for the bar. The bartender raised an eyebrow slightly but otherwise showed no sign of surprise at the quartet. He answered Delta's questions with a faint smile on his lips.

"Naw, I ain't seen no white-looking piano player. Feathers wouldn't hire nobody like that. Yeah. You welcome."

He gave them directions to the second place on Edie's paper, and they trouped out again. They visited five bars in all that night. Edie heart sank thinking about Anabelle playing in any of these places. They were uniformly noisy, the clientele was mostly male. Walking from the door to the bar and back again was like running a gauntlet. Men appraised the women openly and laid bets with their friends on whether ugly was better meat than pretty. The women decided to pack it in after midnight since the drunks were getting louder and more aggressive. They had found one bartender who remembered someone that fit Anabelle's description, but she hadn't been hired, so he didn't know anything more.

"It's a start," commented Delta on the ride home. "At least we know she's down there somewhere. T.J. and I both work nights except for Sunday and Monday. A lot of these places are closed Mondays, so why don't we just plan on popping down every Sunday night for a while—hit two or three and see what we find. Can't promise you anything, Edie, but you might get lucky."

Back in Korba's room in Takoma Park, Edie sat with her head in her hands. She had two searches going, and they both seemed hopeless. Why had she given up her safe Tin Lizzie in Owensville? She couldn't go back, but how in hell was she supposed to go forward? This was a big city. A murder wouldn't even make the newspapers. Korba and her friends were great, but how long were they going to put up with a search that wasn't theirs? She felt Korba touch her shoulder.

"Chin up, Edie, you never know what's ahead," she said. "Here, this'll help you sleep." She handed her a glass of warm milk.

Edie took the glass silently and stared at it.

"Tell you what," said Korba, running her hand through her hair. "I could use an extra hand on the job I'm doing. I know you're good with a hammer 'cause I've seen all that furniture you built. Outdoor construction's not all that different. I can't pay you a whole lot, but it'll keep you busy. Whaddya say?"

Edie closed her eyes and drank the milk in one slow draft. Then she opened them and looked at Korba.

"You're a helluva friend, boss."

3. Out of the shattered reflecting pool

Anabelle's fingers slid over the keys automatically. The club was smoky and noisy, nobody was paying any attention to the music. She was glad she was playing alone. The sounds coming out of the piano seemed detached from the fingers playing them. She couldn't stay in one key for more than a couple of minutes. She would start out playing some old standard she'd been playing for years, get halfway through the first chorus, then hear herself moving from one unrelated key to another. Or rather she'd hear her left hand move through the chromaticisms while her right hand continued sounding the melody plaintively in the original key. Each hand doing its own thing, the way her mind seemed to be going in two directions at once.

This was the third place she'd played in since she left the club on Georgia Avenue. The first one let her go because the bass player couldn't follow her changes; the second one because she'd gotten into a fight with a customer who kept yelling "Play *Misty* for me." She'd finally told him she didn't play that honky shit. No, she remembered, it wasn't the customer she'd screamed at, she'd ignored him. It was the club owner who'd come up and told her to play whatever the goddamn customers asked for. Now she was playing in this dump where the customers didn't request anything, they were too busy dealing or nodding or passing out.

It was hard being black, she'd found. Right after the fight with Jackson and his wife, she'd gone out and gotten herself an Afro, used makeup to bring out black features she'd never noticed she had before. Still, black people saw her as white. All three club owners had given her a hard time about her calling herself black, and every evening she'd heard somebody ask, 'Who's the white chick playing piano?' at least four times.

Anabelle let her eyes wander around the smoke-filled room. The clock over the bar said 12:30, only half an hour to go before she could pack it in. She wasn't sure how she was going to get back to her room on H Street. At the other two clubs, one of the musicians had given her a lift. But there weren't any other musicians here, the club owner wasn't too friendly, and she was pretty sure she couldn't get a cab to come out to this part of town. Her mind veered off the problem as her left hand jumped into yet another key.

"Those some kinda weird changes, lady." A voice materialized at her elbow. "Where'd you learn to play like that?"

The young man was slightly built with a pencil-thin mustache and a small white scar on his left cheek that made his smile crooked. Anabelle continued playing.

"No, I mean it. I like what you doing, I never heard anything like it. I come in here looking for a brother, usually by this time the piano player's having a hard time keeping two fingers going, and I hear these far-out sounds I only heard in my head before. Lady, you oughta be playing in some uptown club where people'd listen to you."

138

Anabelle looked the man straight in the eye while her left hand flipped through several more changes. Her right hand was stuck on a single A-flat, hitting it again and again in an irregular rhythmic pattern.

"I played there already. This where I belong."

The young man cocked his head.

"Yeah, Eddie told me you calling yourself black. I know you chicks who can pass can have a hard time, but playing down here ain't making you blacker. Come on, lady, where's your pride?"

He was angry. The fucker was angry. Here she was, minding her own business, playing for her people, the real people, and this jackass was telling her go play for oreos. Her left hand was thrashing the keys now, hitting notes flat out while her right hand was literally beating the A-flat to death.

The club owner appeared. "You can stop that shit right now. Here's your money. I do better with Two-Finger Juney."

Anabelle smashed the cover down over the keys, grabbed the bills out of the owner's hand, and walked out of the club. On the street she stopped, confused. Her mind was lost in cacophony. Sounds crashed against each other, there were no rests, no silence, only chords that made no sense. The street was dark. Most of the storefronts were boarded over. The only streetlamp was at least a block and a half away. She hadn't even stopped to call a cab, not that one would come.

The man with the scar took her elbow. "I can see what I said upset you. Sorry. Guess I owe you a ride home. I'm gay, if it'll reassure you. But then, you don't have too much choice, do you? You gonna have to trust me."

Anabelle walked to his car with him without saying a word. Her left hand was still jerking as if it had to play out the chord changes of her mind. When he asked her where she lived, she didn't answer. The room on H Street was all mixed up with the room on the third floor of the house on Sixteenth Street. She couldn't remember where either of them was.

They drove through the dark streets in silence. When they crossed the bridge into Northeast Washington, the man with the scar said, "Tell you what, sister. Either you don't know where you live, or you don't want to tell me. Either way, we're not going to get you there. So unless you tell me something else, I'm gonna take you to my aunt's house. Well, she's not really my aunt, she kinda a-dopted me 'cause I'm so cute. She lives in Brookland, and she's got a spare room. Now I ain't doin' this 'cause you black, you understand, I'm doing it because you play real fine piano, too fine to get lost in Anacostia."

As he drove through Northeast Washington, working streetlamps were closer together, and the houses were trimmer with yards and chainlink fences. He pulled up in front of a story-and-a-half frame house on a tree-lined street. A light was still on in one of the upstairs rooms.

"My name's Jefferson, by the way. Might as well introduce myself before I introduce you to my aunt. You don't have to say a word, I know, your name's Annie."

He got out of the car and opened the door for Anabelle.

"Come on, you can't sit here all night. The neighbors'll talk."

He half pulled her out of the car. She was limp, her left hand still twitching but her eyes glazed over. She nodded at him vaguely and let him lead her up the walk. He gave the doorbell three short punches and then began picking at the torn "Jackson in '84" sticker on the front door glass. They heard the sound of footsteps, and then the porch light came on. The door opened.

"Who in the devil...? Jefferson Todd, do you know what time it is? Who you got with you? I told you not to go bringing any of your ofay boyfriends here to spread AIDS."

"Do she look like a boyfriend, Aunt Berta? Your eyesight's failing for sure. This here's Annie, she don't talk much, but she plays real good piano. She needs a place to spend the night, and I knew you'd be looking for a pinocle partner. Seriously, Aunty, the lady's in trouble. She's trying to be black in Anacostia, and I got her fired from her piano-playing job. Now she don't even talk. But she plays piano like nobody you ever heard."

"Well, don't stand there jawing, bring her in. Come into the light, sister, let me take a look at you."

Jefferson gently pushed Anabelle through the door. Her eyes roamed around the room, passed over the overstuffed furniture in the living room to rest on an old upright in the parlour. Aunt Berta, a tall bony woman, folded her arms over her breasts and looked her up and down.

"What's wrong with her? Drugs? Or is she in some kinda shock?"

"It don't feel like drugs to me, somehow. It's something different, but I can't say what. Can she stay here?"

"I guess so. She got any folks? Anybody we can call?"

"I'm telling you, she don't talk. I'm listening to her play these real weird but beautiful chords, then when I tell her she should be playing somewhere better, she says about three words to me, then she flips out. I can check back with Eddie tomorrow and find out where she lives, okay?"

Anabelle heard the conversation through a screen. She kept looking from one face to the other. When the young man left, she let herself be led docilely up the stairs and into a large bedroom. She went through the motions of getting undressed with a half-smile frozen on her face. The chords continued to sound in her head, but they were softer now, and there were spaces in between. As she pulled the hand-stitched quilt over her, she heard her right hand break away from its A-flat monotone to travel on up the keyboard.

Anabelle slept for thirty hours straight. The smell of baking ham drifted through her dreams along with muffled voices and dogs barking. She opened her eyes once to see Berta's head poked in through the door, then she drifted away again. Finally Berta's firm hand shook her shoulder.

"That's enough for now. It's Monday morning, I'm off to my job. I brought you some coffee, there's bread on the counter and leftover ham in the fridge. The clothes on that chair there ought to fit you. I'll be back around five-thirty. If you go out, be sure you lock up—the backdoor keys are hanging on a hook over the kitchen sink."

Anabelle smiled as Berta left the room. The sun was already pouring its heat through the open window. She drank the coffee and looked out into a small backyard with a grape arbour to one side and a neat garden across the back. A large shade tree cast its shadows over the house. She felt calm, calmer than she'd felt in a long time. It was as if she'd set out on a long sea voyage years ago, and the seas had gotten stormier and stormier until somehow a gale had blown her into this safe port.

She looked down at her hands. They were both quiet now, dark against the blue and white of the quilt. She got up and put on the clothes Berta had laid out for her. She spent some time wandering from room to room, holding her coffee in both hands, sipping it from time to time. She looked at the faces in the photographs on the walls, glanced at the books on a shelf, thumbed through the record collection. She found an old Monk recording and put it on the turntable. It was as scratchy and worn as the one Mattie had given her those many summers ago. Mattie, she thought, I wonder where she is now. She listened to the old sounds and began to feel anchored again.

She sat down at the piano and let her right hand roam over the keys. A gentle melody flowed out, moving along with a steady rhythm. She brought her left hand up to add some harmony, but it stayed on an open-fifth drone that lightly added a quiet Latin rhythm. All the sound seemed far away, as if another person in another room were playing them. Eventually she stopped playing and curled up on the window seat. By then it was late afternoon. Some little girls were playing on the sidewalk in front of the house, a group of teenagers stood on the corner and smoked cigarettes. She heard the key turn in the lock and looked up into Berta's broad face.

"Hey, those duds fit you fine. They belong to my grandchild. Did you eat?"

Anabelle looked startled. No, she'd forgotten. She didn't remember when she'd last eaten. Some kind of sandwich in the bar last night. No, it wasn't last night and it wasn't that bar, it was the one before. Hunger jolted her, and she followed Berta out to the kitchen eagerly.

"Well, I had one helluva day shuffling papers. My boss is such a jackass, works himself into a fit every day about three o'clock. Then the rest of us have to scramble, pulling this file out, rushing that one to the print office—in general, covering his ass. If it's okay with you, I'd just as soon pick on left-over ham."

Anabelle nodded and took the plates Berta handed her. Berta turned on the television, and they listened to the

143

news while they ate. Anabelle took slice after slice of ham, not bothering to put them between two pieces of bread. Berta watched her as she ate. When the news was over, she flicked off the TV.

"Are you ready to talk? Jefferson found out your whole name is Annie Jones of no known address. Or at least that's what you told that club owner. You think you can fill me in on any other details of your life? You surely didn't spring full-blown from the banks of the Anacostia."

Anabelle had been enjoying the warmth and safety of the house. But with Berta's question, confusion engulfed her again, her mind drew back. She could see Berta's lips moving and hear the words coming out, but each word was a world unto itself, she couldn't make out the connections between them.

"It's okay, sister. You don't have to talk yet. One of these days, yes, but if it frightens you that much, then it can wait." Berta seemed to be able to see inside her mind. She cleared the table and handed Anabelle a dish towel while she drew hot water into the sink.

The days following were pretty much the same. Anabelle sat and watched the street life all day, waiting to hear Berta's key in the lock. Berta came home, fixed a light meal for them both, told stories about her boss and other people at her office. She seemed content to let Anabelle take her time. They were eating a mess of black-eyed peas on Thursday evening when the phone rang, and Berta left the kitchen to answer it. After a few minutes, she returned, her brows furrowed.

"You got some company coming," she said. "One thing you can say for Washington, at heart it's just another sleepy southern town that loves to hear a good story. I told some people at church last Sunday about how you

144

showed up on my doorstep. So now this women calls, says she got the story from a friend who heard it from her step-niece who heard it from her second cousin's boyfriend's uncle. Says she used to know a jazz musician who played good piano who looked like you, or at least looked like whatever the description was by the time it made all those rounds."

Anabelle looked at Berta, her head cocked.

"Turns out this woman lives right in this neighborhood 'bout two blocks down. Said she'd be right over to check you out, if it's okay with you. I said I didn't think you'd mind."

Anabelle frowned, still trying to make sense out of what Berta was saying. Berta carried the dishes from the table and stacked them in the sink. A few minutes later the doorbell rang. Berta moved across the living room and opened the door. A large muscular woman with steel-rimmed glasses set on a face that made you stand back and take notice walked into the room. Anabelle had followed Berta in from the kitchen and stood, confused this time by what she saw rather than what she heard. The face, the eyes, the whole stance was familiar, somebody she knew, somebody she loved.

"It's her all right, it's Anabelle. Anabelle Webster. I haven't seen her in ten years, but she hasn't changed a bit!"

Anabelle continued to stare at the woman, her brow furrowed. Slowly the corners of her mouth started to twitch a little, and a tentative smile took over her features.

"Mattie," she said softly. "Mattie Dixon." She repeated the name over and over. "Mattie. Mattie Dixon. Mattie."

Mattie put her arm around Anabelle's shoulder. "What's going on with you, Anabelle? Berta says you don't talk, you don't seem to know who you are. What kinda trouble you in, you can't tell people who you are?"

Anabelle laid her head against Mattie's.

"You want to carry her with you?" asked Berta. "She's welcome here. There's room, and she's no trouble."

"Berta, you're one in a million. But she's like kin to me, I've known her since I was twelve." Mattie turned to Anabelle. "You okay? Can you come with me?"

Anabelle's smile kept flickering from her mouth to her eyes and back again. She nodded her head slowly.

"I'm sure glad to know we're neighbors, Berta. Why don't you and your nephew plan to come to dinner on Sunday? Maybe by then we'll have our musician friend talking."

Mattie led Anabelle out of the house. The evening air was warm, and a slight breeze rustled the trees. Two blocks over, she led her into a house identical to Berta's, same living room, same parlour, same upright piano.

"This was modern suburbia in 1922," said Mattie, as she settled Anabelle at the kitchen table and put water on to boil. "You bought your lot, and a contractor came along with his one houseplan and told you you could have it in frame or stucco—or brick, if you wanted to go fancy. The only brick one is next door. The two old ladies who live in it are the sisters of the original owner, a sea captain who wanted nothing but the best. Their fireplace is marble, and they got little electric candelabras coming out of the walls."

Mattie chatted as she fixed coffee for them. She pulled some chocolate cake off the shelf, cut two thick slices, and set them down with the coffee on the kitchen table.

"You think you're ready to tell me what's happening with you? Or do you want me to fill you in on my life first?"

Anabelle put both hands around her coffee cup and

smiled in relief.

"Well now, the last time I saw you was in 'seventy-four or 'seventy-five. 'Seventy-five, I think, because Kijana was eleven. You were just starting to play with some really hot group, remember? And Kijana and I came up to hear you at that club on the north shore. And I was still working in that damn sweat shop, sewing sleeves. So sometime not long after that I got laid off and after my unemployment ran out, I still hadn't found a job. It was a real hard year. I finally went on ADC, we got evicted twice, spent three weeks in a shelter. It was the year of the big snow—the trains weren't running, nobody could get anywhere, much less look for work. I thought I'd had it. I was just about to ship Kijana off to my grandmother who still lives in South Carolina. But then, you never know what's around the corner, do you?"

Anabelle sipped her coffee and played with the chocolate cake. Was it really that long since she'd seen Mattie? How come she hadn't kept track of her? Mattie was continuing.

"Well now, it was just getting into high tech time for the masses. One of the technical colleges started offering an electronics course for high school grads. I aced their little aptitude test and persuaded welfare to send me. That's a whole other story, you can hear that another time. Anyway, I took the course—it was a one-year deal, we never got much beyond the kind of basic electricity they teach boys matter-of-fact in high school. But it made me think there might be something better than another shirt factory minimum wage job where the boss can still tell you, 'You don't come in Saturday, don't bother coming in Monday.'"

Mattie stopped to bite off a big chunk of chocolate cake and then went on.

"So now I've got us this one-room apartment in Dorchester, I'm traveling the Red Line four times a day, taking Kijana to school and then me to school and then back to pick her up and then home to get us something to eat, study 'til midnight, fall across the bed and start all over again the next day. But I graduated—first in the class, too. I was the only woman, the only black and the only one over twenty-five. You better believe nobody was too happy about me taking the honors. But what could they do? The tests were all straight problems—you either got 'em right or you got 'em wrong. I got 'em all right."

She chuckled and got up to pour them both more coffee.

"So anyway, I got my little certificate, got my interview clothes all ready, and I go to their dinky little placement office. I'm rarin' to go. The placement officer hands me a list of job openings for junior technicians. There's a whole raft of them with salaries that look like nothing I've ever seen before. I flip through them and guess what? They're all out on Route 128. 'Got any subways out there?' I ask, 'Any trains?' And the guy smirks at me, 'No, of course not, you'll need a car.'"

Mattie snorted.

"Now with a whole lot of pushing and prodding, welfare'll spring for tuition. But a car? Not a chance. I got my training, I'm hot to go, but the jobs might as well be in Timbuktu. So I'm really pissed now, I'm about ready to toss a bomb when the guy says, 'Did you try the phone company? They don't advertise, but sometimes they hire your kind.' It's 1976 and I'm still listening to that 'your kind' shit. I can't decide whether to smack the guy one or get the information. I think about Kijana, and I ask for the address.

"So I go on over to the phone company. And they look

at me kinda funny, but they're real polite. And they give me their aptitude test. When I pass that one flying, they give me another test—and you can see under their polite smiles they're hoping like hell I won't make it. Now the second test is real electronics, the kind we didn't get to at our dinky little school. But I figure it out and pass anyway. They had to put me on their list, no choice. That was in July. They called in November. They didn't have a test technician job, but they did have a linesman opening, it paid the same as technician, did I want it? Did I want it? Kijana had just had her sneakers stolen, I'd spent the whole day fighting with welfare, I'd of climbed Mount Everest for a real job.

"So that was it. I started out next day climbing telephone poles. Let me tell you, it wasn't friendly at all. We worked in twos, and you better believe who always went up the pole when it was raining or snowing or blowing a gale. And the ladders—heavy as hell, we're suppose to carry them together, but guess who always has his hands full of one screwdriver and one wrench when it's time to take it off the truck. And the language. I heard more about pussies and cunts and what their great big pricks could do to them. That was when they weren't asking me how much I charged for a blow job. The racism was just as subtle. How did I like riding the jungle train to work? Real thigh-slappers, they were. But I kept an image of Kijana in my head and kept my mouth shut. Every two Fridays I'd pick up a pay packet that was twice what I'd ever seen before. Did my five years in Boston, got up to full union scale, then transferred down here. Being black is a lot easier here although being a woman is about the same. I finally made it inside, into a real technician job, so I don't have to climb poles anymore. The pay's good, it goes up every year. I bought this house six years ago, I put Kijana through college. I got no complaints."

Mattie stopped and looked at Anabelle. Anabelle smiled. She was happy to be with Mattie again, happy that Mattie had done so well.

"And you, Anabelle," said Mattie. "How about you?"

Anabelle dropped her eyes in panic. She couldn't remember how she got here, she couldn't remember much of anything about the last few weeks. Her entire life, in fact, seemed a blank. Wisps of memories floated through her mind, but she couldn't catch hold of any of them. She looked at Mattie again, still smiling but with frightened eyes.

"It's okay, Anabelle," said Mattie. "We got all the time in the world. You can tell me tomorrow or next week or next year. You got a home here as long as you need it. Talk or don't talk, I still love you."

Anabelle settled back on the porch swing and pushed herself with her foot. She'd been at Mattie's for almost a week and had not yet been able to speak. She pushed the swing back and forth and watched two little girls shoot their bottle caps onto a chalked pattern of numbers on the sidewalk. One of the girls balanced herself neatly on one foot, the other foot lifted slightly off the ground. Looking like a great bird poised before the flight, she shot her counter with grace, hit the other girl's counter, moved hers to the number five block and shot again.

Anabelle looked at her hands lying quietly in her lap. She hadn't touched the piano since that first day at Berta's. She missed the music. She could still hear it faintly in her head, yet she could not make herself go to the piano. Her thoughts drifted as she watched the children play. She thought about her mother Annie, who she might be, where she was now. She wondered if she had brothers and sisters, if any of them had grown up like her, cut off from her culture. Her culture. But it wasn't her culture. A culture is what you live in, it becomes part of you naturally. If you don't have it, it's not yours. Anabelle's mind wandered on, leaving her lost roots behind. She tried to focus on the immediate past. She couldn't remember much of the weeks before she'd found Mattie. She could sense feelings, but they were distanced. Flecks of pain and anger and even joy seemed to brush her now and then, but she couldn't quite grasp the whole of them.

Then suddenly and clearly, a face came into her inner vision. Rugged squarish, a solid rock—Edie. Edie Cafferty, Vermont, Sixteenth Street...where was she now? Some of the sounds in her head came closer now, jarring her sense of calm with their complex sounds. She started and looked around in panic. Then she saw Mattie coming up the walk with an armload of groceries.

"Mattie!" she called. "Mattie...." She didn't know what she was going to say, so she stopped.

Mattie shifted the bag to her hip and looked at her. "Do you want to talk here or inside?"

Anabelle smiled.

"Out here's fine," she said. "I like to watch the children."

"Let me get the milk into the fridge and warm up this morning's coffee. If it's waited a week, it can wait five minutes longer."

When Mattie reappeared, she handed Anabelle a steaming cup and then lowered herself into the wicker rocker. She sipped her coffee and waited.

"I told you before I was adopted, didn't I?" Anabelle began.

She paused and listened to the sounds in her head. The melody line was quietly searching for a high note, then falling gently into little ripples of sound.

"You remember my folks, always seemed to be doing the right thing for their daughter, like bringing you out from Roxbury to spend the summer."

"Yeah, and I remember how that ended, too," laughed Mattie.

"Well, it was right after that that they told me I was a-dopted. They went through the whole thing of helping me understand why my mother might have given me up so I could have a better life. They answered all my questions whenever I asked them...until I told them I wanted to see my original birth certificate. Then they were evasive, they said it was locked up and couldn't be looked at by anybody, not even them. Which at that time was true. But it was their whole manner that seemed—I don't know, like this was a line I wasn't supposed to cross. It was the same with my music. They gave me lessons and then got real weird when I started playing jazz. They never came to hear me play once. Like black friends were okay so long as they were doctors and lawyers and teachers. But playing in a black night club in Dorchester wasn't what they had in mind for all men are brothers."

"I hear you, girl," said Mattie, rocking herself and sipping coffee. "But your folks weren't the only ones. I met a few of 'em myself."

"Yeah, I suppose so," said Anabelle. "Anyway, I pretty much forgot about looking for my mother until about eight years ago when they were killed in a car crash. I was going through their papers and stuff, and I came across my birth certificate—the one the adoption agency gave them. It looked just like any other birth certificate—my mother's name, my father's name. But I remember at the time, it kind of made me mad, because I knew it wasn't the whole truth. They were my mother and father all right. But I had another mother, too, the one who'd given birth to me. And it didn't seem right that she'd gotten wiped out with the stroke of a pen just because she hadn't been able to raise me. But I was pretty involved with the group I was playing with and didn't have time for a search. So I just filed it away in my mind, something I'd do later."

Anabelle stopped and looked out at the two little girls on the sidewalk who were now doing a hand-patting rhyme.

Juba this and Juba that,
Juba killed a yellow cat.

She listened to the crossrhythms their handpatting made with their voices and felt her own hands yearn to join in.

"Anyway, I finally decided to look for my mother. Or at least find out her name and something about her. I don't know how much you know about adoptees searching for their birth mothers, but I can tell you it isn't easy. It took me almost a year just to find out the name of the adoption agency that had handled the case. And they weren't about to give out any information without a court order. Which I finally got after the third time before a judge. I only got it then because I got some friends to lie for me. But the order finally came through, I informed the agency and headed down here to Washington. I got a ride from a woman who was looking for the daughter she'd given up for adoption and...."

Anabelle stopped suddenly. The music in her head, quiet until now, was drowned out by a thumping rhythm. She closed her eyes, took a deep breath and pushed on. Her voice dropped to a monotone.

"I fell in love with her, Mattie. She was solid and beautiful in a quiet country sort of way. We had a lot of fun together. She was just about as different from me as you could imagine. Grew up poor in Vermont, didn't even finish high school, worked as a bookkeeper all her life. But she understood me, she knew who I was. And she understood my music on a level most people never get to. She was like a home to me. And then...," she struggled to go on.

"And then I found out from the adoption agency that my mother was black, that I'd been born black. I was so angry, I felt like I'd been cheated out of my heritage. I wanted to kill them all—the white doctor, the white hospital, the white agency, my white parents who thought they were being so goddamn white generous...."

"And your white lover," finished Mattie.

They sat still on the porch. A mother's voice called her children home to supper, the radio next door started the six o'clock news. Together they watched the evening fall. Finally Mattie spoke.

"So you got yourself that weird Afro I heard about and tried to find your real self in Anacostia. And the club owners didn't think much of a white chick calling herself black, and they thought even less of the far out music you were playing, according to Berta's nephew."

Anabelle nodded.

"Anabelle, Anabelle, you're just as beautiful white as black, you know. When we say black is beautiful, it don't mean white is ugly. You are whoever you are. You got a gift in you, girl, you got to share it with whoever wants to hear it. That means you play Southeast or Northwest, but you play where folks are listening to you, not in some drug-dealing dive. What you got is special, girl. It don't care about white or black. Yeah, I hear you, you think you missed all that good black growing up. Well, don't think growing up black's all rosy. It's just like growing up any color, some of it's good and some of it ain't. We all got what we got, it was good or it wasn't so good, but that's it, we ain't gonna change it. All we got now is right now. And tomorrow."

Mattie paused. Then she asked, "What about your country woman? Where is she now?"

"I don't know," replied Anabelle flatly. "The things I said

to her were pretty harsh. I wanted to punish someone for denying me my culture, and she happened to be there. She walked out of the club, I'll never see her again."

"Where does she live?"

"Some place in Vermont. She was staying with an aunt in Charlestown. But I don't know the aunt's name or anything."

"Well, that'll have to go on the back burner for a while. You gotta get yourself back in some kind of shape before you try to patch that up, anyhow." Mattie looked at Anabelle. "You sit here a while longer. I'll fix us some dinner. Then we'll talk about what you're going to do with yourself. You gotta get back to your music, but you'll have to think hard about how you're going to do it."

Alone, Anabelle listened to Mattie's words. 'You are whoever you are.' It made a kind of sing-song in her head, and then she heard the crossrhythms of the children's hand-patting rhyme. She got up from the swing and went in to the piano. She put the hand-patting rhythm in the bass and let it outline a series of chords. They moved in and out of several different keys but always came back to home. Then she let her right hand take off. 'You are'—it jumped and answered itself an octave higher. 'You are. You are whoever you are.' The strange harmonies she had heard herself playing at the clubs came back to her. But now she was in control. The right hand knew what the left hand was playing, the two hands affirmed each other.

Mattie came in with an old Stella guitar and started picking out a bass line.

"Go on, girl, play that thing."

'You are,' sang Anabelle's right hand. 'You are whoever you are.'

A nabelle spent the summer teaching. One of the community centers in Northeast had gotten funding to work with teen-age drop-outs. The director, who knew Mattie, persuaded Anabelle to try her hand at involving some of them in music. She hadn't worked with children for years, but she found some of the old ideas she'd had back in her Lower East Side days were still good. The group she worked with jelled at five, two boys barely in their teens and three girls. The boys had signed up for her class because everything else looked boring, they said. The girls all had once had a real interest in music, had played instruments in their school bands but had dropped them along with everything else when they quit school.

The center had some old xylophones and a couple of sets of bongos, so Anabelle started from there. She'd set up the different rhythms and then fire up the battered old piano. Gradually the kids got drawn in. Anabelle went in search of real instruments. By the end of the summer they had a pretty fair combo going—drums, guitar, clarinet, two trumpets and her piano. The director was delighted, the kids were starting to feel good about themselves. Anabelle felt that this was a perfect hiatus for her before she went back to playing at clubs. She was feeling stronger every day.

Evenings, after dinner, she'd sit in Mattie's backyard sipping wine and watching Mattie work in her garden. As dusk fell, Mattie would stop pulling weeds and join her until the mosquitos drove them inside. Then they'd watch a little television together and go to bed.

"We're acting like an old married couple," laughed Mattie as she snapped off the TV after the eleven o'clock news.

They were, thought Anabelle, and it was a safe kind of feeling. A job that kept you busy during the day, good food for dinner and a good friend to spend the evening with. She couldn't remember ever having this kind of quiet, easy life. She'd always lived alone, meeting others in public places, with her room or apartment merely a place to hang her clothes and sleep. She felt she could stay here forever—forget hustling gigs for a living, pass on what she knew to some kids who were interested, and live out her days seeing Mattie across the kitchen table every night.

Unfinished business was pulling her, though. First, there was her mother. She could remember very little of her session with the director of the adoption agency. The woman had been nervous, and she had been impatient. When the news finally broke, she had sat stunned, then she'd exploded and stormed out when the director had tried to do a social work number on her. She'd left without learning anything more about her mother, without learning whether she had brothers and sisters. That was the family business. She'd have to go back to the agency. Not now, but when she was ready.

Then there was Jackson. She'd been playing off and on with Jackson for twenty years, she couldn't leave the relationship broken the way it was. She owed him an apology. Besides, she liked him and his wife and his kids. That was an easier bridge to cross, she knew he wouldn't bear a grudge.

The one who was really on her mind was Edie. She kept seeing her, sturdy and muscular with country warmth behind her eyes. And passion. That was something she'd had only in her music for so many years. To feel that with another woman, to come together, to fuse and separate and fuse again...and then destroy it.

The first two pieces of unfinished business were easy. When she was ready, all she had to do was pick up a phone. But Edie...where was she supposed to start? How could she trust chance to put them together on the same street corner, in the same subway car?

The weekend after Labor Day she finally called Jackson.

"Hey, Jackson, it's Anabelle. You think you can bear to talk to me?"

As she knew, he was glad to hear from her, glad to know she was all right. He wasn't playing anywhere right now, he was getting a deal on to cut a record, he'd know more about it next week. Gloria and the kids were just fine, Gloria got moved up to a GS-11, the kids were all excited about going back to school.

"Did your friend ever find you?" he asked.

Anabelle's heart thumped. "Who do you mean?"

"Jeez, I can't remember her name, but she used to come to the club to listen to you. She was country...real nice, but country."

"When did you see her, Jackson?" She tried to keep her voice even.

"Early June, I think. I thought you might have gone to play in Anacostia, so I gave her some places to try. She

159

called back several times, I guess she went to all of them. Last time I heard from her was sometime around the Fourth of July. I thought she'd found you when she stopped calling."

"No, she didn't find me. Do you have her number? Or somewhere where I can reach her?"

"Let's see, I had it here…not that, that's not it…here it is. Edie, that was her name. The number is 686-5423. Uh, that's in Maryland, I think she said."

Anabelle had a hard time finishing the conversation. She promised to meet Jackson for lunch the next week, and for sure, she'd come to dinner soon. As she hung up, she found her hands were sweating. She had to dial the number three times before she could get it right. Then she let it ring twenty times before she would believe nobody was going to answer. She tried again later in the evening and twice more the next evening. Finally a woman answered, sounding a little grumpy.

"Edie? No, she left with Korba three weeks ago."

"Who's Korba? Where did they say they were going?" Maybe Korba was a new lover. Never mind, she still had to see her.

"Korba, the carpenter. She worked for her all summer. I think they said they were headed for Boston, but I'm not sure. You never know with Korba. She never stays in one place very long. I never had an address for her that was good for more than two months. Usually it's more like two weeks. She finishes a job and moves on. You see her again when you see her, not before."

Anabelle's heart sank. If she had called sooner, she would have caught her. Now all she could do was leave her name and Mattie's phone number. She told the woman it was urgent, if either Edie or this Korba called, please give them the message. Then she hung up and looked out the window. The nights were getting longer again, it was eight o'clock and already dark. The street outside was still with only the occasional sound of a truck backfiring on Rhode Island Avenue. That's two, she thought. Might as well go for the last piece of unfinished business tomorrow.

The next day she put on a dress, brushed her curls into shape, and took the Metro down to Dupont Circle. The agency was housed on the second floor of a brownstone on R Street. When she entered the reception area, the young woman at the desk looked up and a worried look came over her face. She quickly told Anabelle to sit down and hurried from the room. I musta put on some kind of scene, Anabelle thought, to be remembered after all this time. A few minutes later the receptionist returned with Mrs. Johnson, the agency director, in tow. Mrs. Johnson's face was totally impassive as she ushered Anabelle into her office.

"I thought you would probably be back after you'd had some counseling," she said in a smooth controlled voice. She was a small-boned woman with light hair and a smooth bland face. She sat up straight in her chair and held the manila folder very carefully.

"It's not unusual for adoptees to be shocked at the circumstances of their birth," she was saying, "but I'm glad you've returned. I can give you the information now."

Anabelle gritted her teeth. She clenched her jaw and smiled and let the woman continue.

"I have your record right here. I didn't file it away, I was so sure you'd be back. Now, let's see. I have here some information about your birth mother. Not as much as I'd like—we keep better records now. But I hope enough to satisfy your curiosity."

Oh, get on with it, thought Anabelle.

"Your mother was an actress. She was twenty-eight when she brought you in. That's unusual, our clients are usually much younger than that. Let's see, you were two years old. Apparently she had been taking care of you until then, or perhaps her mother had, it doesn't say. But she was the one who brought you in. Hmm, let me see what else. The person who did the intake on her describes her as well-dressed. You were dressed in pink taffeta with bows on it. And you were both clean and well mannered."

The professional unctiousness of Mrs. Johnson and the implicit racism of the record made Anabelle want to jump up and scream. The control these people exercise. All in the interest of other people, of course, never because controlling is something they really like to do. She knew there was information in that file that would give her a real picture of her mother, but this woman wouldn't know it if she saw it.

"May I see the record, please?" she asked.

"Oh, no. These records are confidential. Your court order unsealed them, but the adoption regulation only requires that I read the information myself and use my own judgment to reveal to you those contents that serve the best interest of you and your birth mother."

Anabelle sought to control her voice.

"That's my mother in that record. I have a right to know who she is. You're only telling me the surface. There's more there, and I don't trust you to interpret it for me. I want to see the record myself."

The woman on the other side of the desk smiled. "Of course you want to know all about your mother, it's natural. But really, there's nothing else here of interest. You're fortunate, you know, that this agency has kept its records intact despite all this movement to open sealed records. Some agencies burn their records to prevent disclosure. To some extent, you know, your movement is destructive of the whole institution of adoption. The information given to us by mothers is confidential, it's our duty to protect them. When you come along demanding to see the records, getting court orders to open them to public scrutiny, you are violating the agency-client relationship. You are..."

"Oh, get off your soapbox. That record you're protecting so fiercely is forty-odd years old. My mother isn't the same woman she was then and neither am I. Confidentiality, my ass." Anabelle's voice was rising. "My mother was in trouble. If she waited until I was two years old, she clearly wanted to keep me. When she couldn't manage, she came to your agency. I doubt very much if she gave a damn who you told. And I'm dead certain that if she were here right now, she'd grab that damn record right out of your hands...."

Mrs. Johnson stood up suddenly, holding the manila file to her chest. Her face had turned from professionally pleasant to hard and cold.

"I'm sorry you choose to be difficult. I've told you all I can tell you. Perhaps you haven't seen a counselor, after all. If you'll stop at the desk on the way out, Sherry will give you the names of two very good ones. I suggest you talk to one of them. You clearly have some unresolved hostility toward authority that you need to work out."

"You're the one with unresolved hostility, goddamn it, hostility toward anyone who challenges your goddamn control."

Anabelle tore the door open and ran down the hall. Tears stung her eyes as she stumbled down the stairs. She'd let the woman treat her like a child, she *felt* like a child. It all comes down to control, she thought as she left the building and took in the fresh air. Who's in charge, who can say 'no' without challenge.

Out on the sidewalk she stood shaking, trying to pull herself together. She was as angry at herself as at the agency director. She'd let her temper prevent her from finding out what she wanted to know again. What to do now. She fished in her mind and suddenly remembered a funny old character who had often sat with the band during breaks and talked about Afro-American culture, usually old movies she'd never heard of. He was white with long white hair and a goatee, and he openly bragged that he had acquired his black wife as part of his Afro-American studies. Worked at the Library of Congress, he'd said, called himself, what was it? James Weldon Carruthers. How could she have forgotten a name like that?

She walked quickly to Dupont Circle and slipped into a drugstore phone booth. It only took seven phone calls to track him down, sitting in some dusty archive somewhere in the bowels of the library, she imagined. He remembered her, he was delighted she'd called, he'd be happy to run a check on her mother, he'd call her this evening to let her know what he'd found out.

Anabelle took the bus home and started fixing dinner. When Mattie arrived, she told her what had happened.

"Don't be so hard on yourself, girl. Maybe there wasn't anything else in that folder but some more 'golly gee, look how clean the black folks is.' Anyway, you did find out something. She was an actress, and she held on to you until you were two. That's important."

"Yeah, I don't suppose it was real easy being a black actress in the forties and having a kid, too. I wonder how she managed? Let's see, she was twenty-eight in 'forty-three, how old would she be now? In her seventies, I guess."

The phone rang.

"That must be Carruthers," she said and quickly went to answer it.

Mattie watched her from the doorway as she listened to the other end of the line and jotted notes on the phone pad. After she hung up, she sat quietly, her face a blank, tapping a rhythm with her pencil on the phone. Mattie waited.

"She's dead," said Anabelle flatly. "He found a newspaper clipping from the *Amsterdam News*. She was killed in a plane crash in 1944."

Mattie moved across the room and put her hand on Anabelle's shoulder. Anabelle stared at her notes.

"She was in the chorus of a Broadway musical called *Blackbirds of 1939*. Then he found her name listed among the extras in the movies *Stormy Weather* and *Cabin in the Sky*. They were both made in 1943. I was two years old then, so she must have given me up just before she went to Hollywood. The news story said she was on her way back to New York City when the plane she was in crashed."

Mattie squeezed her shoulder.

"Poor babe," she said. "Poor mama. But still, you gotta be proud. Not everybody gets an obit in the *Amsterdam News*. He say anything else?"

"Only that there was this movie in the thirties that had a light-skinned woman in it trying to pass." She looked at her notes. "*Imitation of Life*. He thought she might have been influenced by it, might have thought that with my light skin I would have a better life growing up white."

"What a set of choices," said Mattie. "She couldn't work as an actress and raise you up decent, and she couldn't raise you at all unless she could work. I suppose white looked good to her from where she was at."

Anabelle closed her eyes and leaned back against Mattie's strong hand. They stayed that way without talking while the light faded. Finally Anabelle stood up.

"I can't cry," she said. "I've only got one way to mourn her."

She went to the piano and let her right hand begin a slow bluesy wail. Soft chords added tension. Mattie pulled out the Stella and started to pick out a bass line. Anabelle followed the wail with her voice, bending the notes like a reed, letting her grief pour through. Her mother was dead. She'd found the missing link, but it couldn't be connected. Only the notes could be connected. Weave them together to make a winding sheet, let the rhythm mark out a cooling board, let the moan follow her to the burying ground. The music continued into the night until Anabelle fell exhausted over the keys.

"God, how I wanted to know her," she cried.

And then let Mattie pull her up and put her to bed.

4. Paths converge, paths diverge

Aunt Flo set the last plate of this morning's dishes into the draining rack and wiped her hands. It was a gray Saturday afternoon, and the light coming in through the narrow kitchen window was fading. She was thinking about Edie. She'd been so delighted when Edie had arrived last spring. After the shock of her mission had worn off, she'd been looking forward to helping with the search. But Edie had left, come back and left again. That's what happens to people you care about, she thought. They're always going their own way. Eight years ago Charlene had gone out of her daily life, and now her only contact with her oldest and dearest friend was a weekly letter. She took the stationery down from the cupboard, pulled a pen out of the kitchen drawer, and sat down at the table to write.

September 3

My dearest Charlene,
  Your trip to the islands sounds wonderful. I know how you love little Anthoula, but it must be nice to get away on your own once in a while. The folk singer you mentioned—did she speak any English? Or are you able to converse entirely in Greek now? What an accomplishment! Your description of the

pebbled beach reminded me of the summers we used to go to Rockport Lodge together. Those vacations were such fun. Do you remember the time we rented bicycles and bicycled all the way to Pigeon Cove? And then we forgot about the time and had to bicycle home at dusk without any lights! I thought we'd never make it. I often wonder what happened to all those women who stayed at the lodge. Do you think they go back every year like we said we would? I got a notice about a reunion last spring, but I didn't get around to going.

You remember my niece Edie. I told you how she had decided to look for her little girl and had found out that the man who took the baby away from her just put her into St. Elizabeth's Children's Home. Well, she called last night and we talked about it a bit. I feel so bad for her. You know, when you and I were trying to figure out what to do about the situation, why didn't it ever occur to us that she could have kept the child? We all could have raised it together. I know things like that weren't done in those days. But then things like you and me living together weren't done either, and we did that. I guess it's all water under the bridge now, but poor Edie seems at such loose ends. She's staying in Washington for a while longer. A carpenter friend of hers is doing some kind of remodeling job down there, and Edie's helping her. Edie always was good with her hands.

Not much else is happening. They hired a new girl at work, so I'm breaking her in. I'm not sure why she took the job, it's just an office assistant job, and she has a college degree. I guess jobs are scarce—or so I've heard.

Give my love to little Anthoula. I can't believe she's having her eighteenth birthday.

Affectionately yours,
Flossie

My dearest Charlene,

I went to the library this morning and looked up your little island in the atlas. The librarian got interested, too, and found me a nice travel book on Greece. When I told her about your folk singer, she got out a book of Greek folk songs and, sure enough, there were eight songs in it from your island of Skyros. I wished I could read music better—there were so many notes. The words were interesting, too. This was my favorite:

I'm no false coin that you can throw me away.

I'm a Venetian florin inside a gold cigarette case.

Now, what do you think that means? If you go to your island again, maybe your friend knows the song.

It's exciting that Anthoula was accepted into the University of London. It certainly speaks well for her English teacher! But what will you do when she goes away? Will they keep you on? Is there some other work you can do for them?

My niece Edie called again last night, and we had a long chat. It turns out that she's been worried, not about her daughter, but about a girl she went to Washington with. The girl disappeared, and no one knows where she is. Apparently this is why Edie has been so down this summer. She seems to have forgotten all about looking for her daughter. I feel a little silly because all summer I've been putting messages for her in the personals—mostly the local papers, the Globes's so expensive I only ran it there once. And a couple of magazines that have missing persons' columns. I expect you'll think I'm just a busybody. But honestly, I have been feeling so guilty for my part in that adoption that I just had to do something. I didn't give Edie's name, though, just my own. And each time I only said Mary Catherine Cafferty—that's the name the orphanage gave her—your biological family is looking for you. So that could mean me, couldn't it? And I really do want to find her.

Poor child, she was taken away from a mother who could have really loved her and then simply put in an orphanage.

I'm running out of room and won't start another page. The new girl at the office is very sharp. I'd better watch out, or she'll have my job. You didn't answer me about what you will do when Anthoula leaves.

Affectionately yours,
Flossie

September 17

Dearest Charlene,

I've been thinking about family these days. I forgot to tell you that when my niece called last week, she told me this strange story about the friend she's looking for. Apparently the girl was adopted when she was an infant, and the adoption agency never told her parents—who were quite well to do and lived in Belmont—that her mother was a Negro. This girl is a jazz musician and has always been close to the colored people. Well, I got to thinking about her and about how Edie wants to find her daughter. Why is it that we put such a value on family ties? We've all been brought up to think those are the most important relations. But I wonder. I'm sixty-seven years old, and I don't think I've seen any of my blood relations more than twice in the past ten years. Except for Edie, I don't really think we care very much for one another. You are more family to me than anyone I know. But family is important, isn't it? I remember feeling so sad whenever Grandma told us about how the first Cafferty came over on a potato famine boat, and both parents died in steerage and all thirteen children got parceled out to different passengers and never saw one another again. So I keep asking myself, what does it mean, family? And the only answer I can come up with is that family means connections, it means people

172

you feel connected to. Because I always have felt like you were family to me. Even when we got so mad at each other that time and didn't speak for nearly a year. Funny, now I can't even remember what we argued about. I guess I'm just a rambling old lady. I do miss Edie. It felt so nice to have her here. I keep hoping she'll come back and stay awhile.

The new girl at the office is a real whiz. They brought in one of those computer machines the other day, and she just sat down and got it to working right away. She said this computer machine would one day make us have a 'paperless office.' If there weren't any paper, what would we all do all day? Anyway, right now the computer is hitched up to a printing machine and seems to spit out paper all day long. It makes a terrible racket.

Affectionately yours,
Flossie

September 24

My dearest Charlene,

I just can't believe what happened today. I'm still in a state of shock. Mr. Bellows called me in to his office, it must have been a little after three in the afternoon. He asked me how I was feeling, and I said fine, and then he said something about the weather. I couldn't for the life of me figure out what he wanted me for. Then he shuffled some papers on his desk and hemmed and hawed and mumbled something about how I was sixty-seven, wasn't I, and I'd been with the company forty-two years. As if he didn't know, his father hired me. And then, Charlene, you won't believe it, he said he thought I had served the company so long and so well that I deserved a rest. And he had met with the board last night, and they had decided that I should retire. He said he realized that they hadn't started the pension fund until I was too old to qualify for it,

173

but they wanted to reward me for my years of service with a little token of their gratitude. And do you know what he gave me? A gold pen! A gold pen, Charlene, it's sitting right here before my eyes. I couldn't believe it. That's why they hired that girl with her college degree. That's why they bought that computer machine. I taught her everything about the business, and she put it all in that machine, and now they're pushing me out the door. I'm so hurt, I don't know what to do. I know I'm two years past retirement age, but I'm still sharp upstairs. What on earth will I do? I don't have any hobbies, and you're so far away. Oh, I don't want to upset you, dearest, but I don't know who to talk to. Edie is still in Washington. I think she hasn't given up hope of finding her friend.

Affectionately yours,
Flossie

September 30

My dearest, dearest Charlene,
    Our letters must have crossed. Oh, I feel so bad for you. How could they do that to you, after all you've given their daughter. Surely there is some work you could do for them, translating or something. What will you do now? Is there someone they can recommend you to for another governess job? Oh, if only I could hold you now, we could be of some comfort to each other. There are so many miles between us. You'll think me silly, but I miss you so much, I wish you were here, we could go out together and tell the world a thing or two. Edie hasn't come back from Washington yet. I'll make this just a note so I can catch the five o'clock post. Keep your chin up, something is bound to come along.

Affectionately yours,
Flossie

Edie eased her truck through the rush-hour traffic. She was barely listening to Korba describing their upcoming remodeling project. She realized she hadn't dropped a postcard to Aunt Flo all summer, she'd only talked to her twice on the phone. She was eager to see her.

She looked at her brown arm resting lightly on the open window. It had been hotter than hell in Washington. Most of the time she hadn't been able to see the nails she was pounding from the sweat pouring off her brow. But she had taken to carpentry like a dyke to a dance floor. She loved the tremor that traveled up her arm when her hammer met a nail square on. Raising a roof actually gave her goosebumps. At first she'd just waited for Korba to tell her what to do and how to do it. But gradually she'd discovered that figuring out where a wall should go was as much fun as putting it up, and she learned to take measurements exactly and translate them to paper plans.

They had spent a lot of evenings in Anacostia with T.J. and Delta, but they'd had no luck in locating Anabelle. Two of the clubs they'd stopped in had remembered vaguely a white woman playing piano. But aside from the novelty of it, they hadn't taken much notice and didn't have any idea where she might have gone after she'd left. As the summer wore on, the ache in Edie's heart subsided into a quiet regret for the lover she might have had. She still had hopes of finding her, but it seemed that by now Anabelle must have forgotten her.

She pulled up in front of Aunt Flo's apartment building and turned off the engine. The grubby street had a nice feel to it, it was almost like coming home. But as her key turned in the lock, she sensed something was not right.

"Aunt Flo! It's only three o'clock. What are you doing here so early?"

Aunt Flo looked up from the newspaper. She was so glad to see Edie, but she couldn't seem to find the energy to stand up.

"Oh, Edie, you're back!" She struggled to her feet. "Here, let me warm up the coffee. Is this your friend that you lost?"

"No, Aunt Flo, this is Korba. She's the one I've been working with this summer. Do you mind if she stays here for a few nights? She's got a remodeling project in the South End, I'll be working with her there."

Aunt Flo rustled the cups and spoons and pushed the dirty plates to one side of the table.

"Your friends are always welcome, you know that, Edie. But the friend you were looking for, did you find her?"

Edie looked away. "No, she's disappeared entirely. I...but you, Aunt Flo. How come you're here in the middle of the afternoon? Are you sick?"

It was Aunt Flo's turn to look away. Her voice dropped to almost a whisper.

"I never missed a day's work being sick," she said, measuring each word evenly. "But they seem to think old age is a sickness. They retired me. They gave me a gold pen."

"They did what?" cried Korba. "They gave you a gold pen? Edie said you'd been working there for forty-odd years. They can't just send you off with a gold pen, that's absurd."

The three of them spent the next several hours hashing over what might be done to the ineffable Mr. Bellows, and where the gold pen might best be put to use. In the end they had to admit that the company had the legal right to force retirement on anyone over sixty-five. And the legal right not to give a pension to someone who was already sixty when the pension plan was brought in to the company. And the legal right to wait until doomsday, if they wanted, before bringing in a pension plan. And the legal right to give a gold pen or a gold shoelace as a token of their esteem. Morality, they decided, is not a deductible expense, and any company has the legal right not to indulge in it. Aside from sneaking down at night and coating the disk drives with honey, there was little they could think of to do for revenge. Other directions had to be looked to.

The next day Edie and Korba were walking along Mass Avenue in Cambridge when Edie stopped suddenly in front of a travel agency. *Come to Sunny Greece*, the poster proclaimed over a smiling young woman standing in front of the Parthenon.

"That's it," said Edie firmly. "That's the solution."

"What is?" asked Korba. "Sunny Greece?"

"Aunt Flo's friend Charlene. She lives in Greece. She's nanny to some rich Greeks' brat. She's Aunt Flo's best friend, they used to live together."

"Boston marriage, huh?"

"I don't know, I never asked her. Well, I almost did once, I was really curious. But it didn't seem like the sort of thing you'd ask Aunt Flo. Anyway, the woman got a small inheritance and went off to Greece a while back. Aunt Flo writes her regularly, and the way she talks about her, I know she misses her. Come on."

Edie grabbed Korba's arm and pulled her into the agency. In a large dingy room, a young woman sat behind a desk surrounded by piles of folders. She was muttering as they came in, trying to extract a single folder from the bottom of the stack.

"How much is a ticket to Greece?" demanded Edie. Before Korba could quite take in all that was happening, they had walked out with a one-way plane ticket to Athens. On the way home, they stopped at a luggage store where they bought a purse, a leather travel case and a complete set of luggage.

"That's the end of the yard sale money," said Edie. "This carpentry business had better pay off, or I'll be back stuffing numbers into spreadsheets. Come on, let's go tell Aunt Flo what she's going to do with the rest of her life."

The travel agent had assured Edie that a passport could be gotten in two weeks, so Edie had booked passage for the third. Everyone scrambled. There was the South End project to get started, and Edie insisted that Aunt Flo buy a whole new wardrobe. Evenings found them cleaning out a lifetime's accumulation of the things that apartments and houses are filled with. Standing in front of her open closet, Aunt Flo wailed, "But they're all still good, there's lots of wear left in them."

"You've been wearing those suits for at least fifteen years, if not twenty-five. And three shiny raincoats are not what you need in sunny Greece."

Edie and Korba sat Aunt Flo down in the rocker and tackled the closet, dumping dress after blouse after skirt into boxes and bags bound for the Salvation Army. Aunt Flo's weak protests—"But I like that one!"—were quickly overruled—"No, you don't, it was just suitable for that damn job." Eventually Aunt Flo got into the spirit and attacked the bureau, tossing out sweaters and slips and girdles—"Lord, how I hated girdles, you just always wore one."

Another evening found them stripping the shelves of knick-knacks and jewelry.

"Uncle George gave me that garnet brooch."

"Uncle George had lousy taste, and so did you if you wore it, but I'll bet you didn't."

"That set of doilies was tatted by my cousin Catherine."

"Occupational therapy, treatment's over."

"Oh, Lord, those silly ashtrays, I thought I threw them out years ago."

"You did, they've come back to haunt you."

A third evening was spent with several cardboard boxes of photographs, all in a jumble with out-of-focus families standing in front of 1947 Fords, small children dressed up stiffly in front of Christmas stockings.

"I always meant to go through them and put them in a scrapbook, but I never did. I don't know as I could tell you who half of these people are...oh, there, Edie, that's your mother and dad when they were first engaged."

Edie took the picture and stared at the young woman with long dark hair dressed in a dark suit. The skirt came almost to her ankles and the blouse had a frilly white collar. She was smiling full face at the camera, her arm linked through the arm of a tall good-looking man who was grinning down at her. She's beautiful, thought Edie. And she's happy.

"Here's another, they must be married now, that's the truck they moved to Vermont in."

Edie's mother was at the wheel, her head sticking out, her right hand reaching over to give a thumbs-up sign.

"And here she is with Iola. And here's one with you in the buggy. This one's your dad just before he shipped out."

He was tall and smiling, his private's hat pulled rakishly over one eye, a little girl in each arm. Aunt Flo passed her a dozen or so more, mostly of her and Iola, a couple of her father with his arms around the shoulders of his army buddies. Edie sat back on her heels and spread the pictures out on the floor. Engaged, married, first child, second, husband going off to war, daughters growing, husband overseas. That's the whole record, her ten years of happiness. More than most people get, she guessed. But what a price she had to pay for it.

"There, that's it, I'll keep these, throw the rest out!"

Aunt Flo brought her out of her musing.

"That's everything, then?" asked Korba.

"Closets, bureau, desk, shelves, there's no place else to put things in this apartment. You girls can decide what to keep of the kitchen stuff, throw out what you don't need, I've no use for it now." She looked around at the bare walls. "Lord, Edie, I can't believe this is really happening to me. I've never been out of New England, let alone America."

"It's about time then. What did Charlene say?"

Edie had persuaded her aunt to telephone Charlene instead of sending a telegram.

"Oh, we both chattered on like a couple of schoolgirls. She kept saying, 'You're really coming,' and I kept saying 'I'm really coming.' Her voice sounded so clear, she could have been around the corner. She said she doesn't have to leave her place until November, so we'll have time to look for someplace to live. There's this little island she's always liked, it's close to the island the family always went to on holiday. She used to go over there by herself. She met a wonderful woman who sings folk songs, and they talk—Charlene says she's pretty good at Greek now. And this woman told her to come and live there. So maybe we'll go there. She says Athen's pretty expensive, but this island is off the beaten track. She thinks we could live like royalty on our social security. Oh, Edie, I'm out of breath again just thinking about it."

"You're all set then," said Edie, looking at the list on the kitchen table. "Your passport came today, you've straightened them out down at Social Security, you've told your landlord about Korba and me taking over the lease, you're all packed. All that's left is to dump these boxes out with the garbage and get you to the plane. What do we do about your mail?"

"Oh, I hardly get any these days. Anything that looks interesting you can open and see if you think I'd want it and send it on. Throw the rest in the trash." Aunt Flo paused. "No, there might be something important. I forgot to tell you. I've been putting notices in the personals for your daughter."

"Notices?" said Edie. "What for?"

"Well, I thought if she still lived here, she might read the personals. And then, there are some magazines that have a missing persons section where you can post a notice for someone, so I wrote them, too. I thought there might be a chance...." Aunt Flo's voice trailed off.

Edie frowned. "I don't think there's much chance of anything happening there. It seems like a pretty hopeless case. But thanks anyway, I'll keep an eye out."

The next week Edie and Korba watched the big Boeing take off.

"That's one of the nicest damn things I ever knew anyone to do," said Korba.

"She's one of the nicest damn persons I've ever known.

I owe her a lot. She's the one who keeps the family con-nections alive. She keeps me up to date on my sister and my brothers and my cousins, even though none of us makes any effort to keep up with each other."

"Well, she's one super lady. I sure hope if she didn't have a proper Boston marriage before, she'll have one on her little Greek island. I like the idea."

"Me, too," said Edie as they climbed into the truck. "Now let's get back to pounding nails so we can keep her landlord happy."

October stretched itself into a magnificent Indian summer. Edie and Korba worked like monkeys until dark every day, taking advantage of the good weather to get the outside work done. The day the radio forecast a coming storm found them working furiously to finish raising the roof. It was hard, the plywood sheets were heavy to maneuver, even with the pulley system they'd rigged. Edie had always been proud of her muscles, but she'd never put her strength to test like this. Now, her shirt soaked with sweat, she felt a buzz every time a sheet slid into place. Nailing them down, she set up a rhythm—one, two, three strokes of the hammer to drive one home and move on to the next. It was after dark when the last nail went in. They stood bone tired, their arms around each other's shoulders, admiring the work.

"I can't believe I squirreled myself away in that dreary office for twenty-five years when I could have been doing this," said Edie.

"And you can't say you didn't have the opportunity. I asked you to help me on a project three years ago," responded Korba.

"I remember. What did I say? Something about how it

seemed too risky a business, you never knew where your next job was coming from, you never knew when you'd get paid."

"That's still true, you don't. But they do, the jobs keep coming, and the checks eventually roll in."

They packed their gear into the truck and drove to a new Sicilian pizza house Korba had just found out about. As they picked over the everything-but-anchovies deep dish, Edie continued her thoughts.

"You know, I've been away from Owensville for almost six months. And it seems like nothing in my life is the same. I thought I was set up for the rest of my life in my little Tin Lizzie, going to that dreary job, working on my house now and then, spending Saturday and Sunday nights at Rosie's. And then I started this trip, thinking maybe I'd be gone a few weeks and come back, and Chad would forgive me and hire me back. Well, no, that's not true, I wasn't thinking anything, I really didn't know what I was doing. I was just going."

"You were looking for your daughter, I thought. What's happened to that, anyway?" asked Korba.

"Oh, I don't know. I don't seem to be doing anything about it. I've been thinking about going back to that adoptees' support group I went to last spring, but I keep putting it off. I dunno, it seems like I can only handle one search at a time, and this one for Anabelle seems easier. At least I know what kinds of places she's likely to be in."

As they left the pizza house, Korba noticed the flashing neon of a night club across the street.

"Hey, there's one we haven't tried yet. Let's go, it'll only take a minute."

Edie stared at the tilted neon martini glass sending blue and pink bubbles up toward the sky. The temperature had begun to drop, and she shivered in her jacket. They crossed the street and went inside. The air was the usual dim haze of smoke and stale beer. The large room was filled with empty tables plus a few with sallow men with sagging bellies leaning over heavily made up women. The band was on a platform at the far end, the pillars hid the piano from view. Half-hearted applause was rewarding the end of a number.

When the new number began, Edie's heart stopped. She moved up closer, staying next to the wall. A waiter tried to show her to a table, but she waved him away impatiently. Now she could see the piano but only the back of the pianist. It was unmistakable though, the thumping bass line, the strange chords that always sounded just right. She dropped onto a chair. Korba sat down beside her.

"That's her? That's your Anabelle? How can you tell, you can't even see her?"

"It's her. It's her music."

Just then the piano player turned and grinned at the drummer who was finishing a roll. The high cheekbones, the deep set eyes, the dazzling smile, the playful look that said, This is me, give me four bars, I'll trade you back. Edie stared, tears just barely forming in the back of her eyes.

"Anabelle," she said softly to herself, "I've found you."

They both sat quietly, listening to the music. It wasn't much of a band. The drummer was a young woman who sometimes dropped a beat, although her solos were pretty solid. The guitarist just noodled, his fingers running up and down the fretboard without much relationship to what anybody else was doing. The fourth instrument, a saxophone, bleated imitation Coltrane, mercifully running out of breath often. As they finished their set to scattered applause, Korba stood up.

"I've got a little niece in Connecticut I haven't seen for a while. They said it's gonna rain for a few days, so I'll be back on Tuesday. I'll ring three times before I come up. Okay? Go for it, babes."

Edie watched as Anabelle walked away from the piano and sat down with the drummer. Anabelle's hands moved in the air, then drummed on the tablecloth. The drummer listened intently, nodding her head. Edie could recognize a lesson in progress. The band wasn't much, but Anabelle would do her damndest to make it better.

The next time the waiter came around, Edie ordered her Jack Daniels. She wasn't sure what to do next. Anabelle looked great, she didn't look like she was in trouble anymore. Edie watched her finish the lesson, drain her beer and head back for the piano.

During the second set, Edie stopped worrying about how to approach Anabelle and lost herself in the music. She hadn't heard any jazz since last summer. Anabelle's playing, as usual, took her out of herself and into another space, a space where all relationships were between sounds, where tensions built up, were dissipated and built up again. Home was there, but everything moved away from it. Just when it all seemed foreign and disconnected, an old familiar chord would tease you into thinking you knew where you were. Then, without warning, the sound would stop, the number would be over.

The band wrapped it up a little after one. The bar was almost empty as Anabelle closed the lid on the piano. She walked over and said a few words to the bartender, then disappeared into the cloak room. She came out with her coat on, said goodnight to the other musicians and turned to leave the bar. Edie still hadn't moved. Her table was over at the far side, not at all in a direct line between the bar and the door. Yet Anabelle, head down, was detouring around the empty tables, coming closer and closer. Two tables away, she suddenly lifted her eyes, saw Edie and stopped. They stared at each other. Edie half rose out of her chair, then fell back. Anabelle moved slowly toward the table. Edie pulled herself to her feet. Anabelle spoke first.

"Somebody better say something soon, or they'll be mopping the floors around us."

Edie dug her hands in her pockets.

"I was just passing by, I recognized your playing."

Anabelle shrugged her shoulders.

"Yeah, well, the band's not much, but it's a job. I haven't played in a while. Are you living with your aunt in Charlestown?"

Edie shifted her feet.

"Uh, I sent her off to a friend in Greece. I'm staying in her apartment with my carpenter friend. You...you're back in Boston?"

"Yeah, I got this gig, it's the first one since...." She stopped. The silence stretched between them. Finally Edie blurted,

"I've got the truck outside. Can I give you a lift home?"

Anabelle shook her curls and then looked directly at Edie.

"Edie," she said slowly. "I'm really glad to see you. I'm staying with some friends in Somerville, if it's not too far out of your way."

She reached out and took Edie's hand. Then she put both arms around her and lifted her off the floor.

"Edie, Edie, Edie, how we've missed each other."

They let go of each other and walked slowly out onto the dark street. Edie led the way to the truck and unlocked the doors. Neither of them spoke until Edie was on Mass

Avenue heading toward Cambridge.

"You'll have to direct me. I always get lost getting to Somerville from here. Or is there any chance you'd rather come home with me?"

Anabelle leaned back in the seat and closed her eyes.

"Well, if you're going to get lost getting to Somerville, I'd say skip it and head straight for Charlestown."

Edie was sweating as they entered the apartment. She'd imagined finding Anabelle a thousand times, but the scenario had always stopped with the meeting. She had never imagined what might happen next. She'd known Anabelle for such a short time and then lost her so quickly and violently that it might have been a story she'd read somewhere. Now Anabelle was here with her in the apartment. Edie ducked into the bathroom, calling over her shoulder,

"I've got to shower off this crud. Make yourself at home."

She washed herself slowly, remembering the long May morning of lovemaking. Anabelle demanded something different, a role Edie'd never played before—lying back and taking pleasure from someone else's touch. It had been exciting, she remembered, but frightening, too. It meant putting yourself into someone else's hands and letting go. Anabelle's hands were graceful, strong and loving. But those same hands had dismissed her angrily—that was the other side of the coin.

When she came back to the living room, Anabelle was sound asleep on the couch, her shoes kicked off and her jacket and scarf in a heap. Edie pulled the quilt off the bed and tucked her in, slipping a small pillow under her head. Anabelle's face, her mouth half-open, looked like a child's.

"Sleep well, Anabelle," Edie whispered and kissed her forehead. The day had started almost twenty-four hours earlier. By the time her head hit the pillow, Edie too, was a-sleep.

Ten hours later, Edie woke to the smell of burning bacon and the sound of a loud "Ouch!" She poked her head out the bedroom door and saw Anabelle at the sink running cold water over her hand. The frying pan tilted dangerously over the side of the stove.

"Guess I'm not much of a cook, huh?"

Edie took a pot holder and picked up the frying pan with its six blackened strips of shoe leather.

"That's what pot holders are for," she said as she set the pan onto the back of the stove. "Picking up the hot handles of hot pots and pans." She reached over and snapped the toaster. "And that toaster hasn't popped in years. I presume you weren't attached to this well-done bread?"

She pulled out the burnt toast and tossed it in the garbage. Anabelle was doubled over laughing.

"It was supposed to be a simple breakfast. A child could have fixed it. And I have to be rescued by a naked lady armed with a pot holder." She wiped the tears from her eyes. "Is there any place to eat close by? I'll treat if you won't mention this mess again."

"There's a McDonalds a couple of blocks from here. The eggs are plastic, but they're not charred. Give me a chance to get something on, and we'll go."

A few minutes later, Edie and Anabelle slid into the plastic booth, set their plastic trays down on the plastic tabletop and stared at the plastic food.

"It's definitely not charred," said Anabelle and started laughing again. "You should have seen yourself, brandishing a red-and-white polka-dot potholder without a stitch on."

"Yeah, well, you looked pretty silly yourself, holding a

189

seared hand under the faucet with smoke pouring out of the frying pan and the toaster. It's a good thing the landlord never installed the smoke alarm on that floor, we'd have had seven fire engines to the rescue."

The easy laughter and teasing brought back a host of sensations left over from last May. The sky was grey and threatening outside the glass wall of the restaurant, but Anabelle's face was sunshine itself. Her dark eyes reflected the good times of the two weeks in Washington, her strong, supple hands, now grasping an Egg McMuffin, flashed excitement.

"Are you working tonight?" asked Edie.

"No, Sunday night's their local jam night. The manager's got a nephew at Berklee who brings the college crowd over. It's the only night they have any business, I think. Why?"

"I thought we might wander up the coast and find a beach to walk on, maybe a clam box still open."

They left the restaurant and headed north. As she drove the pickup up Route One, Edie kept sneaking looks at Anabelle. She seemed the same yet different. She was looking out the window, snapping her fingers and humming, just like always. But her body seemed quieter, her face didn't dart restlessly. Edie wondered if she'd ever find out what happened last summer.

The beach they found was not quite deserted. A woman jogged behind a bounding Doberman puppy, an old man trudged with his head down, hands in his pockets. The sky continued to threaten rain, and the wind had a little bite to it. They walked in silence, watching the little bands of sandpipers dart to the water's edge, peck frantically at the sand and retreat in disarray before an oncoming wave.

Anabelle finally spoke.

"That's me, a sandpiper. Run to the edge of the water

and run back before a wave hits me. My mother was an actress, you know. She was in *Stormy Weather* and *Cabin in the Sky*. Before that she was in a two-bit musical that lasted six weeks on Broadway. Before that she was probably on the Tough on Black Asses circuit—one-night stands in Atlanta and Memphis and New Orleans and every two-bit town in between. She carried me 'til I was two. Maybe that's why I can't stay still for long—I was born in a vaudeville trunk. Imagine, we have the same life—playing for a bunch of drunks, opening a window on our souls and letting anybody look in, free for the price of a drink."

Edie listened. Whatever Anabelle was saying, it was the explanation of what had happened last summer. Anabelle continued.

"I never felt at home much when I was growing up. I felt like some kind of alien from outer space in Belmont. Except for the summer Mattie came out. We had this great big house at the end of this great long driveway lined by great tall oak trees. Everything in it reeked of money. The two people who lived there kept filling it up with more things that cost money—sofas and rugs and freezers full of steaks. Outside there were always a couple of brand new Chryslers and a swimming pool. I never felt like any of it was mine or had anything to do with me."

Edie walked beside her in silence. She knew if she kept still long enough, the point would eventually come out, the ramble would finally come together.

"Music's got connections, though. Even classical music. One chord is connected to another, put all together they make sense. But classical music's got somebody else's connections. With jazz, you make your own. You take the idea, the outline, and you rearrange the dots so that they're connected to you as well as to each other. And, of course, you're connected to some other people who are connecting the dots, too. Sometimes you follow their dots, sometimes you lay your own dots out there and make them follow you. You don't know how you're going to do it until you start doing it. You can take those dots and carry them far away, outer space, if you want, and you alway know how to get back home. Because home is you, you're part of it, you're not standing there looking at it. You're connected."

A lone seagull swooped out of the sky and rested on a wave directly out from them. It raised itself slightly, flapped its wings, and sent its piercing cry out over the water.

"Then the set's over, the dots vanish into thin air, the connections are all broken. You go back to your grungy little room and wait for the next set of dots to connect."

The wind had risen while they were walking, and the steel grey clouds had begun to spatter occasional raindrops.

"You're home for me, Edie. You're a connection that doesn't vanish, you're always there. Even my tantrums don't faze you. You came looking for me in Anacostia, Jackson told me."

"Yeah, well, I wanted to make sure you were okay. I guess I felt...um...I didn't know if you wanted to see me but I thought maybe...."

Edie stopped. She didn't know what she'd thought, she hadn't thought about anything other than finding Anabelle. Now she still didn't know what she thought.

"I want to make love with you again, Edie," said Anabelle. "I want to hold you, I want to be home with you."

By now the rain spatterings had turned into a steady drizzle. Fog had come up over the ocean, the seagulls' cries came from invisible places. Edie's face turned toward Anabelle's, her lips moved to meet Anabelle's, her arms reached out to hold Anabelle. Inside, the little knot of grey pain that had been with her all summer broke its tether, leaving in its wake a disk of spreading sunshine. Tears mingled with rain and wet salt air on both their cheeks.

"Let me come home to you," whispered Anabelle. "Let me come home."

Is it a dream? Is it real? Raindrops strike the window pane, merging tracks, separating, merging again. Flashes of lightning illuminate the face of the apartment building opposite. Two bodies lie on the bed in a pool of sweet exhaustion. Whose arm, whose leg, whose cool moist skin? They have become one, fallen apart, coalesced again. Fingers have explored spiral depths, tongues have tasted fresh salt brine. Sea anemones have opened and closed, their juices drawn from full and succulent petals. The one who was untouched, untouchable has opened her many-chambered nautilus, her explorer has entered freely, has touched the treasure. Deep echoes have resounded off the shells. The one who had put on the sea urchin's spines has let them fall away, revealing soft flesh and fragility to her fisher. Her soft cries have filled the air. Giving over one's body to the other, each has let herself float away, held only by a slender golden thread. Floating, rising, rising, surfacing in an explosion of concentric waves, then letting the golden thread draw one back into the sea, each has found the connection real.

It is a dream, it is reality. The long afternoon stretches into evening. The storm moves out to sea. In the remaining soft drizzle, raindrops still find the window pane and merge and separate and merge again.

The storm had blown the last of Indian summer out to sea, leaving in its wake raw November. In Charlestown, the three women lived in Aunt Flo's small apartment—Edie and Korba on an early-to-bed, early-to-rise schedule, and Anabelle slipping in around two in the morning. Edie and Koba were working on the inside of their building now, sheet-rocking and taping and painting. One particularly wet nasty afternoon with the wind sweeping through the plastic-covered windows, Anabelle burst into the half-finished house waving a letter.

"Knock off, you two," she cried. "I've got good news to share."

Edie and Korba were both up on ladders, their heads and shoulders covered with grey dust.

"Okay by me," said Edie, "my fingers are numb. Come on, Korba, it'll still be here tomorrow."

"Be with you in a second. I'm gonna finish to the corner."

Anabelle was standing first on one foot, then the other, unable to contain her excitement.

"Look at this," she said, waving a letter in Edie's face.

"I can't read it that way," said Edie. "You better just tell me before you explode."

"Jackson's arranged a tour of Japan! Six months, he wants me to go with him."

"That's great," Edie said carefully. "When do you go?"

"This winter, Edie, first of January. And you're going with me, as my business manager. What do you say?"

"Business manager? I can't do that, I don't know anything about being a business manager."

"Oh, come on, you know numbers, you're an accountant. That's all it is, managing money."

"I'm not an accountant, I *was* a bookkeeper. There's a big difference. Anyway, now I'm a carpenter. I don't want to do books any more." Edie wasn't sure why she was so reluctant. She wanted to be with Anabelle, but....

"I don't see the difference, you still know numbers. Edie, the tour's for six months, don't you want to be with me? We'll have a great time. You'll be finished with this project, it'll be like a honeymoon for us. Then we'll come back, and you can be a carpenter again."

"What's up," said Korba, joining them. "Can we go get some pizza while you two jaw?"

"Anabelle wants me to go to Japan with her this winter."

"Sounds great. We'll be finished here in about six weeks. I'll be ready for a vacation myself. Think I might go to the Bahamas for a coupla months, stretch out in the sun."

"But I've never been out of the country before."

"Neither had Aunt Flo, and she's living in Athens now. You don't have to wait till you're sixty-seven, you know, you could start right now."

It was a sobering thought. Edie had such a nesting instinct. She had not been consciously thinking about the future with Anabelle, but it had been at the back of her mind. The idea of six months in a foreign country began to seem attractive.

195

"Do I have to eat raw fish?" she asked, as they entered the pizza house.

"Edie, the Japanese have the best steaks in the world. You can eat red meat until it paralyzes you. I'll eat the sushi."

During the next few weeks, Edie did a lot of thinking as she painted walls. Her life with Anabelle was not easy. She loved her, there wasn't any doubt about that. But she found her unpredictable, and that was unsettling. Six days a week she went to work, came home, ate dinner, watched a little TV and went to bed. Around two or three in the morning, Anabelle would crawl in beside her and wake her up sometimes to make love. Then they'd sleep until six when Edie would get up and go to work again. That much was steady, a routine, a familiar kind of life. Sundays she never knew what might happen. She often made plans for the two of them to go out to dinner and see a movie, but just as often those plans were tossed aside with a sudden decision by Anabelle to drive down to the cape, for instance, and walk a stormy beach. She always felt swept along with these changes of plans, plans that seemed to spring full-blown from Anabelle's head. They would be eating breakfast, and Anabelle would simply start talking about going as if they'd been planning together for weeks. Unable to resist the force of Anabelle's energy, Edie always felt pulled along like a child. She was often relieved that Sundays came only once a week. Seven days a week in Japan with Anabelle would be something else.

"Just when I think my life is settled, it turns upside down again." Edie was trying to voice some of these thoughts to Korba as they sat at the kitchen table and sorted through Aunt Flo's mail one evening. "Here I was getting into married life again, and suddenly I'm making plans to go to a place where they don't even speak English. How'll I read street signs, they don't use letters? Here, you want a subscription to *Women's Circle?*" She shoved a fat envelope across the table to Korba. "Aunt Flo sure gets a lot of mail for someone who said she wasn't expecting any. Look, here's a letter from my sister. Maybe I'll find out what she's doing in Aunt Flo's next letter."

"You could write her and find out for yourself, you know," said Korba.

"I don't write letters, I can't spell."

"That's no excuse. Who cares if you spell xenophile right? Who cares if you know what it means? She's your sister, for godsakes. When did you last see her?"

"At my mother's funeral twenty-odd years ago."

"And you never phone her, you never write? How do you stay in touch?"

"Oh, she and Aunt Flo correspond. Aunt Flo tells me about what she's doing and I guess tells her what I'm doing."

"Well, I think you ought to take her address off that envelope right now and write her a letter. This evening, as soon as Anabelle leaves. I'll wash the dishes. No TV until you finish."

"Oh, my god, I'm gonna be a kid writing a Christmas thank-you. 'Dear Grandma, Thank you for the very nice handkerchief. I had a very nice Christmas. For presents I got a new blouse, a new skirt and two pairs of socks.'"

"Who's writing Christmas letters?" asked Anabelle as she emerged from the shower.

"Edie is. A pre-Christmas letter to her sister. Hey, Edie, this isn't a subscription notice, it's a couple of envelopes addressed to a box number at the magazine. Handwritten, looks like a child's scrawl."

"Maybe it's a new kind of promotional gimmick," suggested Anabelle. "Go ahead and open it."

"Which one, there're two."

"Either. Go on, let's hear."

Korba tore open the top letter and started to read out loud.

"'Dear Box 1756,'" she began. "'My mom saw your ad in this magazine she was reading at the laundromat. Boy, was she mad. She started yelling about how families aren't nothing, we don't need nobody but just ourselves.'"

"Oh, my god," said Anabelle, moving quickly to stand behind Edie's chair and put her arms around her shoulders. Edie sat stock still, her face drained of color. Korba looked puzzled, turned the sheet over and read the closing signature.

"It says it's from your granddaughter," she said, looking up with a question on her face.

"Go on," said Anabelle. "Read all of it." She bent over Edie and kissed her cheek. "It's okay, babes. Whatever it says, we're ready for it. Don't worry, I'm here."

Korba continued. "'I don't agree with her. I never had any family except Mom. She's okay, but everybody else at school has brothers and sisters and grandparents, and some of them even have fathers. Last week we were suppose to write an essay on one of our grandparents. I made one up and got an A! I'll send it to you. Are you my real grandmother? Where do you live? What do you look like? Why did you give my mom away? My name is Ocean, but everybody calls me Oshi. How do you like the way I spell it? I think it looks Japanese. My best friend is Japanese, her name is Kyoko. Your granddaughter, Oshi.'"

"Here's the essay," said Korba. She took the second sheet of paper and read. "'My Grandmother by Ocean

Free. My grandmother was an Indian princess when she was a little girl. Now she is an old woman with long gray braids and wrinkles on her skin. She is tall, and her hands have funny brown spots on them. She talks Indian talk when she is with her friends, but she talks English to me. Last week my grandmother took me and my friend Kyoko up Grouse Mountain. She showed me a secret place where only Indian women used to go. She said they came there when they had their period. I asked her if I could come when I got my period, and she said, yes, she'll bring me again. My grandmother tells stories about long ago. She tells me about all her sisters and how they used to plant corn together. Her sisters are my great-aunts. Her father was a famous warrior and so was her mother. They are my great-grandparents. I am their great-granddaughter.' "

Korba stopped reading. No one spoke. Finally Anabelle said,

"You were looking for your daughter, but your granddaughter found you."

"How'd she do it?" asked Korba, still puzzled.

"That magazine has a missing persons column. People can put ads in asking for information about anybody they want to find."

"Oh, yeah, Edie, remember your Aunt Flo said something about putting some ads in some magazines," said Korba. "Let's see where she's from."

Korba squinted at the envelope.

"There's no return address and the postmark is smeared. Van…Vancouver, B.C."

Edie still hadn't said anything. Anabelle squeezed her hand.

"Go on, Korba, read the other one."

Korba torn open the envelope.

199

"'Dear gram, May I call you gram? If you're really my grandmother, then it's funny to call you a box number. I didn't put my address in my last letter because if my mom found out I was writing you she'd kill me. She threw the magazine in the trash can, but I went and got it out again. I took eight dollars from her wallet last night, and today I got myself a box at the post office. It was easy. I guess taking her money was stealing, but I'm going to babysit for Carol when she has her baby, so I'll pay her back then. I want to tell you about me. I'm ten years old, and I'm four foot three. My hair is sort of red, and I have green eyes. My name is Ocean because you could see the Pacific Ocean from where I was born. It was in a dome on Vancouver Island. I don't remember that place much. I do remember the commune on this island in Desolation Sound. I like the name Desolation Sound. My mom and I lived there when I was four or five. We left when the woman died. She was having her baby and got sick, and the motor wouldn't start in the boat. They finally got a fishing boat to stop and radio the coast guard, and they sent a helicopter to take her to the hospital, but she died anyway. So did the baby. I didn't mind leaving, the chickens had all died, too. We forgot to feed them. Now we live on Powell Street in Vancouver. Our apartment is right over a Chinese restaurant. The lady there gives me egg rolls sometimes when I come home from school. My mom works at the fish packers. She doesn't get off 'til six, so I have lots of free time. I play with my friend Kyoko, she lives two blocks over. Well, I better close now. Please write to me. My address is Ocean Free, P.O. Box 879, Vancouver, British Columbia 2B76H1. I'm a Canadian, but my mom's American. What are you? Your granddaughter, Oshi'"

The three women sat without talking. Anabelle finally

broke the silence.

"That granddaughter of yours sure writes a four-handkerchief letter, Edie." She blew her nose.

"Jeez, Edie, she's some enterprising kid," said Korba. "You can write to her at her own box number."

"What about her mother?" Edie finally spoke. "My daughter?"

"Well, it sounds like maybe she's had some hard times," said Anabelle. "And after what you found out about her childhood, she's bound to be suspicious of family. All you can do is write to her daughter and hope she comes around later. Oh my god, it's after eight. The set starts in half an hour. Listen, Edie, I'll finish up early, I'll be back by one. Then I'll hold you. Korba, take care of her until I get home." Anabelle phoned a taxi and flew out the door.

Edie and Korba sat quietly for a while. The upstairs apartment sounded like a bowling alley with the kids getting ready for bed. Finally Korba said,

"So you'll write your granddaughter tonight instead of your sister. Here's a pen and paper, I'll clean up."

Edie took the writing things and sat for a long time. What do you say to a ten-year-old granddaughter you didn't even know you had? All this time she'd been thinking about her daughter, knowing in her head she was thirty-two, but never imagining her as someone who might have a child. Edie'd never thought of herself as a mother, much less as a grandmother. Grandmothers were old and had wrinkles and grey hair, just like Oshi wrote. She had a few crowsfeet around her eyes, but otherwise her skin was smooth and her hair still the same reddish brown she'd always had. Red hair—Oshi had it, too. She seemed pretty bright for a ten-year-old. And gutsy. Getting the magazine out of the trash can, stealing the money for a P.O. box. Edie knew where those impulses came from. She finally picked up the pen and started to write.

Dear Oshi,

Yes, I am your grandmother. I am not an Indian princess although my great-grandfather called himself a meti so I guess I have some Indian blood in me. I am not tall either, but I have reddish hair just like you. It comes from my dad's side of the family. They were Irish. Back in the nineteenth century they left Ireland because the potato crops failed, and they didn't have anything to eat. They settled in Boston, and that's where my dad grew up. My mother's family was English and Scots and French Canadian. It was her grandfather that had the Indian blood in him.

I didn't want to give your mother away. I was pretty young though and before she was born, I signed some papers I didn't understand. I took care of her until she was almost four months old. Then a lawyer came and took her away from me. I'm sorry she doesn't want to hear from me, but I can understand. Maybe you and I can get to know each other, and later she'll want to meet me.

I'm sending you $10 (American). Change it at the bank and put the $8 back in your mother's wallet. It's not right to steal even though sometimes it seems like the only way. I did it twice myself when I was carrying your mom. I didn't regret it, but I did pay the money back.

You can call me what everyone else calls me—Edie—or you can call me gram. My love to you.

Edie Cafferty

When she finished the letter to Oshi, Edie picked up another sheet of paper and wrote:

Dear Iola,

The return address is Aunt Flo's, but it's your sister Edie writing. I forwarded your letter to her in Athens where she's staying with her friend Charlene. Her address is 22 Kantartzi Street, Athens, Greece. They retired Aunt Flo from Allied Imports, and Charlene stopped working for the Greek family she was living with. So they may both go live on an island together. I expect she'll write you herself soon.

I'm a carpenter now. We're just finishing a big remodeling job, and I may go to Japan after that. I'd like to come visit you in Seattle. We have a lot to catch up on. Aunt Flo has told me about your life, but I'd like to hear myself. Write to me here and tell me when's a good time.

Love,
Edie

F ive days before the new year found Edie and Korba painting the last wall of the last room of the townhouse. They walked from room to room, Korba looking for any missed detail, Edie admiring their handiwork.

"This calls for a big celebration," said Korba. "Where do you want to go? Did you get a hold of Rosie?"

"She's coming down late this afternoon. I thought we could all go out to dinner and catch Anabelle's show. The club hired a name band for New Year's, so this is her last night there. I told her to meet us at that Italian restaurant in Cambridge. We can clean up here."

In one of the shiny new bathrooms, Edie showered and changed slowly. The new year was just around the corner, the tickets to Japan were bought, and she kept having flashes of resistance to going. She'd gotten two more letters from Oshi and one from her sister. Oshi's mostly chattered about herself and her life, but she also mentioned in each letter that she was working on her mom, she thought she might be able to tell her soon. Oshi told her that her mom still used her commune name, Juniper Free, but that she had decided to be Oshi Cafferty, if that was all right with Edie.

Iola's letter had hit Edie almost as hard as Oshi's. There had been over twenty years of indirect contact only, but when Edie read the letter, she felt like she'd picked up a thread dropped yesterday. Iola was someone she'd slept in the same bed with, shared secrets with, sought shelter with from her mother's anger. Iola had led a completely different life from Edie—marriage, children, a split-level ranch house in suburbia—but that life style didn't affect Edie's feelings at all. She found it hard to believe she'd neglected her for so long.

Both connections were pulling her. She longed to see Iola and to relive some of their childhood memories. If she stayed with her in Seattle, that was only a stone's throw from Vancouver, in case Oshi's mother came around. Or even if she didn't, Edie might be able to see Oshi.

But there was Anabelle. She hadn't talked to her about any of this. She was afraid of Anabelle's anger, afraid she might not understand, might think Edie didn't love her. And she did, she wanted to be with her. They'd had so little time together. In Japan they could wander around during the day, she could listen to Anabelle play every night, they could make love without one of them being half asleep. Yet....

Rosie and Anabelle were standing on the sidewalk outside the restaurant scanning the menu. Edie hugged Rosie, glad to feel her sensible bones. They went inside.

"So tell me about your granddaughter," said Rosie after they'd given their orders. "Did you ever imagine our Edie a grandmother? Tough-as-nails stonedyke, buying us drinks and getting a little drunk every few months. Now she's not only got a daughter we never heard about 'til last spring but a granddaughter to boot. What's she like? How'd you find her?"

205

"Aunt Flo put an ad in the missing persons column of this magazine," said Edie. "According to Oshi—that's short for Ocean, she was born in a commune—anyway, she says her mom was reading the magazine in the laundromat, saw the ad, went on a tear about families and how she didn't want any part of them, and threw the magazine away. Oshi fetched it out of the garbage can and wrote to the magazine. They forwarded her letters to Aunt Flo. We've exchanged quite a few letters, but she still hasn't told her mom. She got herself a P.O. box so her mom wouldn't find out."

"Pretty determined kid, huh?" remarked Rosie. "Sounds a little like her grandma."

Their orders arrived. Edie continued between bites.

"She spent the first five years of her life living in communes in the backwoods of British Columbia. I guess those kids are pretty independent. Now they live right in Vancouver. Life doesn't seem to be very easy for them. Her mom works as a fish packer and has had a string of loser boyfriends. Oshi says she thinks men are dumb, she's gonna be a lesbian when she grows up."

"No kidding. A stubborn lesbian. You've cloned yourself, Edie. So how does all this fit in with the trip to Japan?"

Edie looked down at her plate. "I'm not sure. I...."

"It's about time you started being sure. The plane leaves in five days."

Anabelle's voice cut through the air like a sheet of ice. Edie blushed, looked up and started to speak.

"Anabelle, it's hard. I want to go with you but...."

"Don't give me that hard shit. It's simple, either you go or you don't go. Life's full of decisions—this one or that one, her or the other one, me or your so-called family."

Anabelle's thin smile barely showed her set teeth.

"Uh, is this something Korba and I should step outside for?" asked Rosie. "Sounds like you two have some things to work out."

"No, no, stay for the show!" Anabelle's voice was rising, her hands flashed anger. "Edie just can't make up her fucking mind. She hasn't bothered to keep in touch with her sister, hasn't even seen her in more than twenty years. Now, with a chance to spend six months in Japan with me, she's thinking she can't wait to go visit her. We've barely seen each other, pass like ships in the night, and she's getting ready to dump me for family she just remembered she had yesterday."

"That's not fair!" protested Edie. "I want to be with you, it's just that...."

"Stop it, you two," broke in Korba. "Edie, what's going on? You haven't told me anything about this."

"You're not the only one she hasn't told. Fortunately, I've got a sixth sense, I can tell what she's thinking even when she doesn't talk," said Anabelle. "Otherwise I'd likely learn she's not coming with me when I got on the plane alone."

"Anabelle, calm down," said Rosie. "We can't talk about it through your anger. Here's coffee, let's all take some deep breaths and try to work this through."

There was silence as the waitress served the coffee. Then Anabelle shoved her chair back violently and stood up.

"There's nothing to work through. She's made up her mind, she's just too chickenshit to tell me about it. I gotta get to the club, let her tell you two and y'all can tell me."

Anabelle swept out of the restaurant, leaving a cold chill in her wake.

"Edie," said Rosie, "I know you from way back. I know your no-talking moods. But Anabelle's right. You've got to talk about it, make your decision and tell her. It's not fair to keep her on the hook."

"I know, I know," mumbled Edie. "I just realized when she said that, that I *have* made up my mind. I kept putting off the decision. I guess I'm afraid of her anger. But I do love her, I want her... but I want my family, too. Why can't I have her and my sister and my granddaughter, too? I don't want to have to choose between them."

"You don't have to," said Rosie. "But if that's what you're trying to do, you better be damn careful how you do it. Come on, talk, let us know what's going on in your head."

"Okay. I've gotten these four or five letters from Oshi. I've sent her some. We really seem to connect. I've never written letters before in my life—that's why I never wrote Iola before. Now I find I just sit down with her letter and think about her and start writing. I realize it's only six weeks since I found her, I don't even know what she looks like except for the red hair and a blurry photograph she sent me. But she's real important to me."

Edie paused and drank some coffee.

"It's the same with my sister. It's true I haven't bothered to keep in touch with her, just let Aunt Flo tell me what was going on with her. Then, the night I wrote Oshi, I wrote to her, and it was real easy. When she wrote back, I started remembering how much we cared for each other when we were kids. We sorta were going our separate ways when I was a teenager—she was into boys, and I was into jazz. Her life's been real different from mine— marriage, family, house in the surburbs. But I find I've got real strong feelings for her. I want to reconnect. She's invited me out to Seattle, stay as long as I like. She says there's plenty of carpentry available, I could work...."

"And what about Anabelle? The romance cooling a little?" asked Rosie.

"No, no, it's not. I keep falling more in love with her every day. I know she thinks I resist her a lot. And I do. She has a way of just sweeping you along with plans that come out of nowhere, and I find myself resisting just because I haven't been a part of the planning. I guess I feel a little that way about the trip to Japan. It's her trip, I'd just be coming along. It would make every day like Sunday, going places, seeing things, but always on her time. It's exciting, but...."

"But it's not really you, you don't have any control," finished Rosie.

"I can't believe you're thinking about not going with her," said Korba. "You're in love with each other, you've hardly seen each other, you've got a chance to spend six months together—a love affair and a honeymoon like we all dream of. Edie, where's your noodle? Your sister'll still be there when you get back, Oshi's not going anywhere. You can send her things from Japan, she'd like that, she's nuts over Japanese."

"I know. I can't explain what I'm feeling. Something is pulling me to Seattle. Right now. I want to set up a life with Anabelle...but I want to see my sister now. I want to be close to Oshi, I want to be there if my daughter can be persuaded to let me meet her. I feel like I'm being pulled in two directions, but Seattle's pulling harder. I don't know. I want Anabelle to understand, I want her to wait for me. Or rather, come back to me when her tour's over."

"Well, the only way you're going to get that is by talking to her," said Rosie. "You should have been sharing this with her from the start. Maybe it's not too late. You've got five days, maybe the two of you can go off together somewhere. And talk, Edie. You can't clam up. The lady's sharp, she knows what's going on. It hurts both of you when you don't talk. Let's go catch her first set at the club. Then Korba and I will go stay with a friend of mine in Cambridge. Here's her phone number, in case you need us."

They left the restaurant and drove to the club. The set had just started. Edie recognized Anabelle's angry mode of playing in the brittle chords and harsh bass line. She was scared, really scared she might lose Anabelle. Her last words at the restaurant—'Y'all can tell me'—had been spoken in that mock black accent that Edie still heard occasionally in her nightmares.

At the end of the first set, Rosie and Korba left. Rosie kissed Edie's cheek and whispered, "You can do it, Edie."

Edie watched Anabelle get up from the piano. Instead of looking around the crowd for Edie, she threw herself down at the first table, leaned back in the chair and closed her eyes. Edie wasted precious minutes trying to think what to say. Finally she made her way over to the table.

"Anabelle, I love you."

Anabelle opened her eyes.

"Yeah, well, I love you, too," she said slowly. "But that's life, sometimes things don't work out. You got to do what you got to do. People go their separate ways all the time. Leavetakings are a dime a dozen."

"No, Anabelle. I want to make a life with you when you come back from Japan." Edie spoke clearly and firmly. "I want to hear you say that our connection is strong enough to survive six months of you in Japan and me in Seattle. I want you to care that much."

The words coming out of her mouth surprised Edie herself. Anabelle looked at her long and thoughtfully. She, too, heard something new, and she didn't know quite what to do with it. She got up, still looking at Edie. Then she turned quickly and went to the piano.

Edie's heart pounded throughout the second set. Anabelle's rhythms were jagged, her harmonies strange. The band had a hard time following her. When they did, the music was incredible. Mostly things fell apart, though, and they ended the set before one.

Anabelle went into the cloak room, and Edie waited, swirling her bourbon. Suddenly, out of the corner of her eye, she saw Anabelle's coat on the way out of the club. She's not waiting, she's leaving without me! she thought. Grabbing her jacket, she made a break for the door and hit the sidewalk just in time to see Anabelle disappear into a cab. Across the street was another one. Edie dodged the late night traffic and jumped in.

"That taxi, that yellow cab, can you catch it?"

The cabbie squealed a U-turn and accelerated. Twice she thought they'd lost her, but her cabbie was good, barreling through just-red lights and rounding turns deftly. In front of South Station, Edie saw Anabelle moving quickly toward the station doors. She threw a ten dollar bill into the front seat and was out the door before the cab had stopped.

"Anabelle!" she yelled. "Anabelle, stop! Wait for me. Let me talk to you!"

Anabelle turned and fixed a cold pair of eyes on her.

"It's too late for talk, Edie. You can't have everything. You've made your choice. Now let me go."

Anabelle walked quickly through the doors. Edie ran to keep up.

"Anabelle, I love you, I want you. Wait for me. Let me see my family, then I'll come to you. Anabelle!"

Anabelle kept walking, head high, eyes straight ahead. When Edie tried to take her arm, she shook her off. At the ticket window she said,

"Round trip to Washington and hurry. I want to catch the One-forty-five.

Without looking at Edie, she said, "I'm going to Washington. There's no point in spending the next five days saying goodbye. This is goodbye enough."

The ticket clerk pushed a ticket out to her.

"Track forty-five, you can board now."

Anabelle took the ticket and headed for the gate.

"Anabelle...."

Tears were stinging Edie's eyes, Anabelle was a blur moving away from her. At the gate, Anabelle stopped and said flatly,

"Let go, Edie. You can't have everything. Go to your family, Let go of me."

Then she was gone, through the gate and onto the train. Edie stared numbly at the No Visitors Beyond This Point sign. Farther down the platform, the conductor called, 'All Aboard!' The train started moving. Edie stumbled out of the station. She couldn't believe she'd lost Anabelle. Again. And this time out of her own carelessness. Somehow she got a cab, gave directions to the apartment and eventually fell onto the bed. She lay there numbly for several hours, not thinking, not feeling, not being. Then she fell asleep.

Edie dreams. I've written a postcard to Oshi, but it needs a stamp. I scrounge around behind the seat of the truck and find fifteen cents. There are long lines at the post office—except for one window, a child-size window where a woman sits smiling. I show her the postcard and slide the dime and nickel across the counter. Still smiling, she shakes her head and tells me that the stamp costs sixteen cents. I go to the bank to get some money, but there are long lines there, too. When I finally get to the counter,the teller carefully counts out ten twenties and hands them to me. I tell her it's too much. She smiles and picks up the key chain that I've left on the counter and starts to take off a key, telling me I have to return the key, it's for the lock box. I put my hand over hers and say, No, that's mine. We lock eyes, she continues to smile. We each pull at the key chain until it breaks, scattering the keys onto both sides of the counter.

Before Edie opened her eyes, she felt the empty bed beside her. How many times had she felt a newly empty bed? But this time she was not going to accept it, and she didn't need Rosie to tell her. Rifling through Anabelle's things, she found her address book and dialed a number from it.

"Hello, is this Mattie? This is Edie Cafferty. Is Anabelle there? ... Okay, tell her when she wakes up that I want to talk to her. I'll call this evening after dinner, okay? ... Thanks."

Then she dialed the number Rosie had given her.

"She wouldn't talk to me, Rosie. She left the club without me and took the train to Washington. I just got off the phone to her friend there. ... Yeah, you don't need to tell me. I'm gonna call tonight and every night until we talk. ... Yeah, don't worry, I'm not gonna let go. You on your way back to Vermont? ... Okay, I'll let you know. Thanks."

Edie spent the rest of the day sorting and packing things. She knew pretty much what Anabelle was planning to take to Japan, the rest could stay in a box in the closet. Her own stuff was minimal and fit into one suitcase. Korba came in and gave her a hug.

"What are you going to do?"

"I'm going to my sister's. But I'm going to see Anabelle first. She has to see me before she goes, I've got her ticket. And there has to be a way we can each do what we have to do and still have each other. Dammit, you've showed me how to be a carpenter, how to love what I do for a

213

living. I don't want to go back to diddling figures just to be with her. And if she travels for a living and I like to stay home, why can't we still be together whenever we can be and the rest of the time make our own lives? Why not, Korba?"

All the formless thoughts of the past weeks were tumbling out of Edie's mouth. No longer confused, Edie finally knew what she wanted. How to get it was another thing. But she was sure going to try like hell. She picked up the phone and dialed Mattie's number.

"Hi, it's Edie again. Can I speak to Anabelle? ... Oh. ... Well, tell me what she's saying, what she's planning to do. ... Okay, tell her this: I'm going to call her every evening. She has to see me, I've got her ticket. And tell her I love her, nothing's changed about that. ... Thanks, Mattie."

"What's happening?" asked Korba.

"She won't talk to me. She won't talk to Mattie either, except to say that it's over between us. She's jamming right now with a couple of the kids she worked with last summer. Maybe that's a good sign."

Edie spent the next four days getting herself ready. She changed her ticket for one that gave her stopovers in Seattle, so that she could visit Anabelle if Anabelle'd let her. She called her sister to let her know when she was coming. She wrote letters to Oshi and Aunt Flo. And one to Anabelle.

Dear Anabelle,

This letter writing is still new to me, but I'm going to try to write you how I feel. I love you, that's first. I want to make some kind of life together. You're a jazz musician, and a lot of your life is traveling. I'm a carpenter, and I like to make a home. Why can't we make it so that you can live your life and I can

*live mine and we can still be connected? It seems like it ought to
be possible, but we have to talk about it. I want to see you before
you leave. I just changed my Japan ticket so that I can go to
Seattle first. I'll stay with my sister for January and February. I
want to come visit you in Japan in March or April, if you'll let
me. Just when would depend on Oshi and her mother.*

*I'm sorry I couldn't tell you this before. I didn't know myself
what I wanted. Now I do. I want you and I want my life, too.*

Love,
Edie

The night before Anabelle's plane was to leave, Mattie
finally gave Edie the message she was waiting for. Anabelle would see her for the one hour between her flight
up from Washington and her flight to Tokyo.

Edie was ready hours before Anabelle's plane was due.
She changed her shirt three times, trying on the two new
ones she'd bought and finally settling on the worn blue
denim she had always been most comfortable in. She
pulled open a small box and looked at the earrings she'd
bought on Newbury Street the day before. Lapis lazuli,
the store clerk had told her. The stones were small and
delicate, the blue was deep and wonderful. Edie could see
them already hanging against Anabelle's dark cheeks.

Finally it was time to go. At the airport, she paced up
and down in front of the flight information screen. The
plane from Washington was due in at one-ten; the flight
to Tokyo was scheduled to leave at two-oh-five. Her eyes
darted between the airport clock and the flights-arriving
list. How could the Washington plane be late, it was only
an hour and a half away. Every minute that passed was a
minute lost, precious time with Anabelle squandered because some ground crew in Washington couldn't get it
together.

By the time the arrival was announced at one-forty-five, Edie was frantic. Then she saw Anabelle, her face set in a frown, her dark eyes sweeping the reception area. Edie stood perfectly still and let the eyes move past her and then back to lock with hers. The airport bustle receded into faraway static. Anabelle stood still. Edie moved to her.

"Flight four-ninety-three for Tokyo now boarding at Gate eleven."

There was no time to talk, no time for anything. At the gate Edie handed Anabelle her ticket and the small white box. Anabelle stood back and, still frowning, looked deep into Edie's eyes. Jostled on every side by embarking passengers, the two women were motionless. Anabelle reached out and touched Edie's shoulder.

"I dunno, Edie. We were good together. But now...."

The flight attendant tapped Anabelle gently on the shoulder.

"It's time to go."

Edie held her breath. But Anabelle didn't finish the sentence, she only shrugged and turned away. Then she was gone.

Edie stood on the observation deck and watched the plane taxi down the runway. The wind whipped icy gusts under her collar, tears froze on her face. The plane moved ponderously, paused for a moment, then gunned its way into the air. Edie watched it until it disappeared into a cloud.

5. A good tree has deep roots and wide-flung branches

The Flowers of Hawthorne steeped three days in Wine and afterwards distilled in Glasse, and the Water thereof drunke, it is a Soveraigne Remedie for inward tormenting paines, which is also signified by the prickles that grow on this Tree.

—Coles, 1657

Holding her face up to the soft morning drizzle, Juniper Free dragged the laundry cart down the paper-littered sidewalk. She always laughed when Vancouverites complained about gray skies and fogged-in mountains. She loved the rain, she liked the sound of car tires on wet pavement, the feel of her long red hair plastering itself to her face. She took long strides, enjoying the smack of her rubber boots coming down in the puddles. She'd been lucky to get them and the yellow slicker at the Sally Ann yesterday. Two bucks for the boots, three for the slicker and a dollar more for a handknit sweater for Oshi. Inside the laundromat, she sorted the sheets and shirts into one washer, the jeans and sweatshirts and towels into another. She was almost glad she'd lost her job last week, it was such a luxury, not to be doing laundry on a Saturday morning with everybody else vying for the machines.

As she started to toss in a pair of Oshi's cords, she felt a lump in the back pocket. Damn kids, she thought, you just can't train them to empty their pockets. The envelope she pulled out was dirty and crumpled. She was about to toss it into the trash can when the name on the return address caught her eye: Edie Cafferty. Juniper sat down on the hard bench, stunned. Who the hell was Edie Cafferty? But she already knew. It was in this very laundromat that she'd seen the message in that women's magazine last fall from the family of Mary Catherine Cafferty. Oshi must have fished it out of the trash can and written. That's why she's been so secretive these past months, she thought, that's why she's had been yapping about grandmothers. The little sneak, she's already found her grandmother, she's trying to manipulate me into approving it. Juniper realized she was shaking. She suddenly saw Edie as a monster, dumping her in an orphanage, then ripping back into her life thirty years later trying to win over Oshi. She jammed the envelope into her slicker pocket and shoved quarters into the machines. A tight vise had started to grip her chest.

Juniper got through the rest of the day by scrubbing holes in the torn linoleum floor and scraping the winter grime off the windows. She spaced out, letting the rhythm of the work take over her mind and body. She was sitting at the kitchen table sorting the laundry when she heard Oshi on the stairs. The envelope lay on top of a stack of Oshi's underwear.

"Hi, mom, guess what?" Oshi burst in and threw her schoolbag in the corner. "Our class gets to go to the a-quarium next week, you gotta sign this permission slip and give me a dollar...." Her eye fell on the envelope. "Uh-oh, spaghetti-o!" She retreated a couple of steps. "Guess I'm in for it now."

"Don't try your cute TV lines on me, you little sneak." Juniper spoke through clenched teeth. Her stomach was in knots. Oshi grabbed the envelope and stuffed it into her pocket. She stamped her foot.

"Mom, I told you not to mess with my private stuff in my room."

"And don't think you can brazen it out." Juniper's hands gripped the edge of the table. "That was in your pants pocket that you threw in the wash. I didn't read it. I don't want to. I don't want to know the woman. She dumped me in an orphanage and went on about her merry business. She's nothing to me. And she's gonna be nothing to you either. You've got such big britches, you think you're all grown up and can do as you please. But I'm still paying the rent and putting the food on the table, not that woman. She can't have you."

"Mom!" Oshi put her hands on her hips, but her lips were quivering. "It's not like that. She's neat. She writes neat letters. Anyway," she pushed her lower lip out defiantly, "she's coming to see me this weekend. It's all planned. She's gonna meet me in Strathcona Park."

Juniper felt the floor tilt under her chair. Oshi was all she had. She knew she could survive any disaster—losing a job, getting evicted, being disqualified from unemployment, getting kicked off welfare. But without Oshi it wouldn't be worth it. Oshi was all she had to live for. She heard herself scream as she buried her face in the laundry. Oshi came around the table and put her hands on Juniper's shoulders.

"Mom." Her voice was soft and pleading. "She's not like you think. She didn't dump you in an orphanage. She told me how it happened. This man came and took you away from her. She was only sixteen. Come on, Mom, she'll be here Saturday. I want you to meet her. You'll like her. She's my gram."

Juniper's shoulders heaved. She turned around on the chair and held Oshi tight.

"You're all I've got, baby. I'm the one who raised you, not her. I know it's not easy not having any money. But I'm doing the best I can."

Oshi put her two hands on her mother's face. "Mom, I'm not going off with her. She's only coming for Saturday. Then's she's going back to Seattle. C'mon, come with me and meet her. You'll like her."

Juniper blew her nose and pushed the hair out of her eyes. She took Oshi by the shoulders and held her at arms length.

"Sorry, kid," she said, her voice steady again. "I got a little carried away there. You're right. She's probably a nice lady. But I don't want to meet her. I guess if you want a grandmother, then you can see her. But I don't want a mother. I don't care if it wasn't her fault I grew up in an orphanage, I'm not going to meet her. You can spend three hours with her on Saturday. You'll have to get Carol to go with you. Tell her I'll mind the baby. I'm not taking any chances on you going alone. If you're not back in three hours, I'll call the police. Now, give me the envelope so I can copy her address, just in case she gets any funny ideas."

Oshi extracted the envelope from her pocket and handed it to her mother.

"I promise, Mom. I'm supposed to meet her at noon. I'll be back by three. I'll go ask Carol now."

Oshi ran out the door. Juniper picked up a towel to fold and let the tears run down her cheeks.

Saturday morning, Edie's pickup moved through the March landscape. Early morning fog shrouded the mountains. She kept glancing over her shoulder, waiting for Mount Baker to appear out of the mist. Less than a year ago she had put her truck on the interstate to Boston. Now she could hardly remember her life back in Vermont. What she had done all those years she couldn't imagine. Looking back, it seemed like an endless procession of weekday numbers punctuated by weekend whiskey. When she'd set off to find her daughter last April, she'd had no idea what she might find on her journey. Well, she'd found Anabelle, loved her fiercely first as a friend, then as a lover. Then she had lost her, not once but twice. In the two and a half months since she'd watched Anabelle's plane disappear into the clouds, she had gradually come to resign herself to the consequences of her choices. She didn't regret the choices—connecting with Iola again, being close enough to visit Oshi, striking out on her own as a carpenter. What she regretted was that Anabelle had forced the choice. She missed her, she could still feel her touch. A small glimmer of hope continued to burn in her heart.

The rich delta farmland of lower British Columbia gave way to suburbs. Edie crossed the bridge into Vancouver and eventually picked her way through downtown to Strathcona Park. Oshi had drawn her a map of the park with all the trees clearly marked and a red-jacketed, red-headed Oshi waiting at the swingset. Edie pulled her truck to a stop and looked around. Yes, there were the swings...and there was a little girl in a red jacket. A teen-aged girl was with her. Edie climbed out of the truck, her hands so sweaty she had trouble holding on to the door handle. By now Oshi had spotted her and was running full tilt toward her. Edie stood uncertainly on the sidewalk as Oshi ran to her and threw her arms around her.

"You gotta be Edie, you got a truck and red hair!" cried Oshi. "Come and meet my friend Carol, she's the one I babysit for. My mom said she had to come with us. Carol," she yelled, "this is my gram, her name's Edie, that's her truck."

Carol was a pleasant looking young woman with long

braids down her back. She glanced nervously from Oshi to Edie and said,

"Juniper's a little worried about Oshi going off with you by herself. She asked me to come along."

"Fine with me," said Edie. "Where do you want to go?" she said to Oshi.

"Can we go to Stanley Park and feed the swans? I'll show you the seawall, and then maybe we can get some fish and chips."

Oshi grabbed Edie's hand. The three of them climbed into the truck. Edie followed Carol's directions, and soon they were watching the spring mating rituals of the ducks on the lake. The early morning fog had lifted, leaving only a few wisps clinging to the lower edges of the north shore mountains. The sun was bright and, although the day was still chilly, buds were beginning to form on the trees. Oshi was telling Edie about something that had happened at school.

"...so these two big bullies, Rodney and Joe Chin, were marching around the playground bragging about how they tripped May Yow into a mud puddle. They said her dress flew up and there was a hole in her panties. So Kyoko and me snuck into the art room, and we painted these signs that said 'Kick me in the' and then we drew a picture of a naked butt. And we got safety pins, and while they were in the lunch line, we pinned them to their jackets. They didn't feel a thing. So all through recess, the other boys kept running up to them and kicking their butts. So they got into fights with everybody and got sent to the principal's office, and then...."

They were walking along the seawall by now. Oshi broke off her story suddenly and pointed out into the bay.

"Seals!" she cried. "Look, there they are. There're three of them."

Edie's eyes followed Oshi's finger and finally made out three brown heads bobbing in the water. She'd never seen seals outside of a zoo.

"I swam with some seals once," Oshi was saying, "when we lived on the island. This pack of seals came in real close, there were whole bunches of them. We took off all our clothes and jumped in and swam right out to them, they weren't scared of us at all."

"I thought you said you were only five when you lived on the island. Could you swim then?"

"Sure, I learned to swim when I was three. Most of the kids didn't swim on the island, though, 'cause the water was too cold. But my dad called me a sissy if I didn't go in every day, so I got used to it."

"Where's your dad now? Do you ever see him?"

"Uh-uh. He stayed on the island when Mom and me left. Then he stopped being a hippie. He came to see us once when I was seven. He looked so funny. He had his beard all shaved off except for this teeny little mustache, and his hair was all short and slicked down, and he was wearing this silly suit. It was really weird. I think he used to give my mom some money for me, but he doesn't anymore. I asked Mom if I could go visit his parents when we had to write that grandparents essay in school, but she said they didn't want to know about me. That's when I decided to make up an Indian grandmother. But then I found you, and I don't have to make up one anymore."

Edie caught her breath and bent down to give Oshi a hug. Oshi hugged her back, and then wiggled free, crying,

"Look! We're all the way around the seawall. The fish-and-chips stand is right over there."

She started to run and then stopped short.

"Uh-oh, I forgot, it's too early. They don't open 'til May."

She came back and took Edie's hand to console her.

"You'll just have to come back then, it's the best fish and chips ever."

The warmth of Oshi's hand spread all the way through Edie's body. Is this what you miss when you don't have kids, she wondered. Or are there so many struggles in raising them and keeping them fed and clothed and getting them to behave themselves that moments like this get lost? She'd been listening to Iola's tales of raising teenagers, the endless fighting to get them to pick up after themselves, to take a little responsibility, to stop assuming their mother was a servant at their beck and call. Carol's voice broke into her thoughts.

"It's two forty-five. We'd better go."

Back at Strathcona Park, Edie dug in her pocket and pulled out the pocket knife her dad had given her in one of his rare moments of communication.

"Here," she said to Oshi. "This belonged to your great-granddad. He used it when he was about your age to clean fish with. You have to be careful with it, it's real sharp, and it doesn't have a safety catch."

Oshi took the knife and fingered the smooth bone handle.

"Oh, wow," she said. "Wait 'til I show this to Kyoko. Maybe my mom will show me how to clean a fish with it."

Edie saw Carol glance nervously at her wrist watch. She bent down to give Oshi a hug. Out of the corner of her eye, she saw a woman with a baby standing at the edge of the park. The woman was short and slender and had long red hair falling to her shoulders. Her eyes locked with Edie's. A shock ran from Edie's head to her toes as she looked into eyes that could have been looking at her out of a mirror. Oshi felt Edie stiffen and followed her gaze.

"That's my mom!" she cried and tore out of Edie's arms. She raced toward Juniper yelling, "Mom! Mom! Come and meet Edie. We fed the swans and we saw three seals and she gave me a knife and we're back right on time like I told you!"

Carol ran and took the baby out of Juniper's arms and walked quickly out of the park. Edie stood for a moment and then started to move toward mother and daughter. In her slow dream walk, Edie watched Juniper allow herself to be pulled along by Oshi. They were ten feet apart when they all stopped, unable to move farther. Oshi stepped away from her mother and looked from face to face. No one spoke. Finally Juniper broke the silence.

"I don't need a mother," she said evenly. "But Oshi wants a grandmother, and I have to go along with it for her sake."

Edie took a deep breath.

"I don't think I need a daughter, either," she said slowly. "But I do want the connection. I didn't want to give you up. You were important to me then, and you're important to me now." She paused and then went on. "I guess I can understand if you don't want to know me but...." Again she stopped, not knowing what else to say. This was Sarah—Mary Catherine, Juniper now, but still Sarah to her. This was the woman she'd left Vermont for, this was her flesh and blood. She could see that Juniper was on the verge of tears. She wanted to hold her and tell her it was all right. Instead she heard herself saying,

"You weren't the only child that ever got ripped out of her mother's arms. There were lots of others like you, like me. Those people managed it because I was young, and I didn't know how to fight. But you shouldn't let the people who did it keep us apart."

She stopped, shocked at the fierceness of her words.

227

She added softly,

"I guess I'll have to accept it if you say no, and I'll care for you anyway.

"Oh, shit," said Juniper. "Oh, shit, shit, shit, shit, shit." She fumbled in her pocket for a tissue and blew her nose.

"That's sixty cents!" crowed Oshi. "You said 'shit' six times, that's sixty cents for the bad-word jar."

Edie laughed out loud. Then she held out her two hands and stepped forward. Juniper took one hand, Oshi took the other, and the three of them made a circle. The spring sun shone down on them as they stood awkwardly looking at each other. Suddenly Juniper jerked her hand out of Edie's.

"I'm not ready for this!" she cried and ran out of the park. Oshi's face fell. She clung tightly to Edie's hand. Edie pushed her gently and said,

"Go with her, Oshi. I'll be in touch."

Oshi gave Edie a quick hug, and then ran to catch up with her mother. Edie watched the two of them disappear down the street. Then she walked slowly back to her truck.

The sky changed from bright blue to fiery red to deep purple as Edie drove back to Seattle. She put her mind into a no-think mode, but a long string of images flowed through anyway. Korba tossing her a hammer...Rosie pouring her a whiskey...Aunt Flo handing her a bowl of Irish stew...Iola reading a newspaper...her Tin Lizzie with smoke coming out of its chimney...Anabelle with her head bent over the keys...Oshi tossing popcorn to the swans...Sarah/Juniper standing at the edge of the park.... She was bone tired when she pulled the truck into Iola's garage. The house was dark, it was Iola's night for bowling. Edie groped through the entryway and flipped on the kitchen light. A small brown package lay on the counter. Edie turned on the burner under the coffee pot and sat down. Finally she reached for the package and turned it over. Foreign stamps, her name in small cramped letters, no return. She opened it slowly and took out of folded piece of paper. A thin gold chain with a small blue stone attached fell out of it. Edie looked at it for a long time without moving. Then she unfolded the paper.

> *Lapis lazuli.*
> *Yes. So as not to forget*
> *the rare connexion.*

She smiled and turned the paper over. A scrawled 'Come soon' was followed by the address of an Osaka Hotel.

"All right," she breathed. "All right, I will."

She turned off the coffee and went to stretch out on the floral patterned sofa. She held the blue stone to her cheek and fell asleep.

Edie dreams. I'm floating down the White River on a large raft with some other women. It's warm and sunny, and the raft floats lazily. Then the current is faster, the raft breaks into pieces, the river splits into several branches. My piece of the raft floats down one branch, and I lose sight of the others. A great blue heron lands on my raft, and the raft starts swirling. I lie flat on my back watching the sky turn around. As the raft shoots out of the rapids into calmer water, the heron flies away, flapping its great wings. My raft bumps into a tall wooden structure. I climb onto it. It's part of an old covered bridge, but the sides are gone. I climb up as far as I can go and look around. I can see the other rafts, some still floating, some fetched up on shore. The great blue heron is perched in a hawthorn. The pink blossoms are gone now, and the berries are ripe. I look at the hammer in my hand and nail down a loose board.

About the Author

Ellen Frye grew up in rural Ohio, went to college in New York City, and has lived in Washington, Boston, Chicago, and Vancouver. She is the author of *The Marble Threshing Floor: A Collection of Greek Folk Songs* and has written for *off our backs*, among other journals. Formerly a music teacher, she now works as a technical writer and lives in a three-story house in White River Junction, Vermont with two pianos and two cats.

Other Titles Available

Order from New Victoria Publishers, P.O. Box 27, Norwich VT 05055.

Something Shady by Sarah Dreher ($8.95)

Travel agent/detective Stoner McTavish becomes an inmate in a suspicious rest home on the coast of Maine to rescue a missing nurse.

Stoner McTavish by Sarah Dreher ($7.95)

The original Stoner McTavish mystery introduces psychic Aunt Hermione, practical partner Marylou, and Stoner herself, off to the Grand Tetons to rescue dream lover Gwen.

Promise of the Rose Stone by Claudia McKay ($7.95)

Mountain warrior Isa journeys to the Federation to confront the ruling elite. She is banished to the women's compound in the living satellite, Olyeve, where she and her lover, Cleothe, plan their escape.

Runway at Eland Springs by Rebecca Béguin ($7.95)

Anna, a pilot carrying supplies and people into the African bush, finds herself in conflict when she agrees to scout and fly supplies for a big game hunter. She turns to Jilu, the woman who runs the safari camp at Eland Spring, for love and support.

Radical Feminists of Heterodoxy by Judith Schwarz ($8.95)

Revised edition of the history of Heterodoxy, the club for unorthodox women that flourished in Greenwich Village from 1914 through the 1930s. Original photos and cartoons.

In 1860, women's rights activist Emily Faithful founded Victoria Press, an all-women print shop in London, England. Her tradition was revived in New England with the establishment in 1975 of New Victoria Printers and, in the following year, New Victoria Publishers. Although New Victoria Printers no longer exists, New Victoria Publishers carries on, publishing the finest in lesbian feminist fiction and non-fiction.